Prelude

My name is Trevor McCoy II. I began writing this with much reservation, even deleting it twice before resolving to tell my story. Every couple hundred words I copy the new text to my thumb drive and delete any traces from my hard drive. The story needs to be told, regardless of the risk.

I am 20 years old and it's 2038. Thirty nine years since the beginning of the great pandemic. Grandpa, the senior Trevor McCoy, has told me stories since I was 8 or 9 about the pre pandemic days. Stories about the United States of America, what it was like when he was 48 years old and the dreaded Covid–19 pandemic hit our country. He repeats, every time we meet, never repeat these stories and discuss this with anyone else, EVER. And then he tells me another story he experienced or stories his Dad told him dating back to the 1980's.

He tells one story that took place in 2025. He was secure in his placement with the Agency. He was a journeyman plumber and supervised another 5 plumbers under the Agency.

They did new installation and repairs to houses, workplaces, and entertainment venues. One of his workers that he was especially fond of, a man about his age, socialized and met frequently with other couples that despised the Agency. They had no guns, no plans to protest, or any plans to be public about their dissent. Any of these violations would result in an immediate PVR (Personal Value Rating) rating deduction , probably a loss of their current jobs, and a loss of monthly value credits. Monthly value credits (MVC) are the incomes that the agency establishes a base line minimum pay for each profession. The amount is based largely on each professions value to the society, amount of skills and training, and a persons PVR (Personal Value Rating). Getting caught dissenting in any way can be a life changing event. If any one in their group was caught with a weapon, especially a firearm, they would go to a detention facility or even worse, a prison. Their daughter who was the same age as my Dad, about 19, had been recruited by the Agency when she was 12 years old in the seventh grade. Almost everyone aspired to work for the Agency. She attended a gymnastics class that was closed to the parents. The Agency used venues like this to recruit, install loyalty, train, and elevate the recruit's as they matured. She was first indoctrinated and brain washed in the Agency values, then vetted, sworn to allegiance, and then entered the Agency underground as an Agency informant. Agency undercover informants had a high PVR as they became field agents and ultimately became independent of their families. They can count on better Monthly Value Credits, more expendable income, better housing and privileges.

As part of this girls training at about age 16 she was taught how to plant bugs, listening devices, and make recordings. She was very good at this and got her class 1 certificate in this area. Typically an Agency undercover agent would start their career with a 60 to 70 PVR barring any other violations of the rules, like theft, speaking against the Agency, or becoming pregnant or causing a pregnancy with out a mating card and a marriage license from the Secretary of Relationships and Marriage. Turning in dissenters, organizers against the Agency, Black Marketeers, anyone disobeying the rules of the Agency, received immediate recognition in their PVR and a subsequent increase in their Monthly Value Credits. Grandpa goes on to describe the atmosphere in the late 20's. Nobody really trusted anybody. Everybody was always looking over their shoulder. Never say what you really feel in public. You may want to take a machine gun to the Agency board but your life will be much better if you advocate for the Agency.

The Republic of America would not even exist if it wasn't for the brave Agency founders, many passed away now, with many of their children and heirs in control. This girl, I never got her name, actually bugged and recorded a meeting at her house of her parents and three other couples discussing the loss of freedoms. The fear of reprisals, stories about detention centers, and how they could improve their lives. The discussions were about how to get back to the constitution, a government, democracy, freedom of speech, due process, freedom of travel, and wealth accumulation. The right to choose your own life mate, and the right to orchestrate your children s education and future. For a field agent reporting with good evidence, these violations in the late 2020's was equivalent to saving life's, breaking world records in swimming, or inventing a new medical cure in the eyes of the Agency leaders. Typically a graduating Agency undercover investigator would receive a 60 to 70 PVR which, would correspond to a nice suburban house, a nice city flat, furniture, electronics and about 6000 Value Credits monthly for housing, food and luxuries, savings, and vacations. This is easily in the 70%–75% maximum income range.
But adding a confirmed break up of an anti-Agency group would earn you another 5 PVR points which then would result in a higher monthly Value Credit (VC) for life.

And, added to your resume that the dissenters were your own family members proved your loyalty and allegiance to the Agency.

Her parents and co-conspirators got 6 months in detention after being tried without representation. They worked on farms while they were reeducated and duly warned about any repeat offenses. Upon their release their PVR was reduced by 20 points and their Monthly Value Credits reduced equally. They lost the privilege of their 4 bedroom stand alone house and were relocated to apartment housing. It will take them 10 years to regain their meaningful careers, stature in society, and have enough monthly credits to afford a vacation or any luxuries.

The Agency undercover agents are everywhere. For most bright people it makes more sense to cooperate and do the best you can given the situation then draw any attention to yourself and your family.

Chapter 1 – Early days of the Agency

There are some allowable books on the subject of the Agency. They can be found in libraries, schools, book shops, and on-line. I borrowed a copy of "The truth about the Agency" from one of my parents friends. I read it in one night and returned it promptly. The author, a Hudson Institute Scholar, wrote it in 2025 and several thousands of copies got into distribution before the Agency was able to collect them. The author spent many years in detention and reeducation. The allowable books say the Agency was formed in the late summer of 2024 just weeks after the assassination of Donald Trump. Grandpa Trevor says from a couple things he has read and discarded, and other friends have confirmed that the Agency began meeting about 2018. The Agency was formed by about a dozen filthy rich, successful, powerful men and woman and met secretly in places like Alaska, the Caribbean, and Europe. Always away from the eyes of the press and on lookers. They have been compared to the Bohemian club of the 20th century. Rich industrialists, politicians, educators, retired and active military brass, and philanthropists, would join by invitation only to discuss world affairs, politics, the arts, and society. They met in secrecy at the Bohemian Lodge on the Russian river in Sonoma county. Many deals, programs, political decisions were made from here.

It's believed that the Agency's origins were a couple or more of it's founders discussing the distention, riots, deteriorating education system, wokness, racial issues, and foreign affairs just prior and following the Trump Presidency. The riots and lack of local government intervention disturbed them terribly. Before long they had begun to realize that the entire structure of society could fall apart. It is said of the original board of the Agency that the combined net worth was well over one trillion dollars. Most were so successful they had turned over their primary roles of CEO of their companies. They remained on the Board of Directors and took up new projects. Almost all were generous philanthropists.

Some had hobbies (new businesses) exploring space, sports teams, and pet projects around the world. After reaching 5 billion or 80 billion in net worth they had no need for more money. They all had in common a love for the USA, gratitude that free markets and capitalism gave them the opportunity to succeed. Their egos were stoked giving back. They felt it was their duty and had a strong dedication to insuring their employees future. This is why most of them never sold out completely. They wanted their partners and employees treated fairly forever. They were long past the point of taking advantage of every situation for their own pocket books.

Secretly they all liked Trump for his guts, policies, willingness to take on the swamp and his resilience as he took on fire from every direction for over 5 years. Even Martha Presley who Trump branded as "Horse Face" in the 2016 primaries agrees he did a great job. They agreed he was brash, arrogant, misogynistic, had some ethnic bias's, but, they could sleep at night when it came to the threat from overseas adversaries and domestic strife.

Biden wouldn't lift a finger or take the smallest risk to put down a country or a violent political organization. He had no control of the strongest country in the world. He was a puppet, and a poor one at that. The Agency board members didn't want their respective dynasties destroyed, but more than that they owed this country a great debt of gratitude and thanks. During good times, there was no better place than the USA.

If they couldn't come to the call of replacing chaos with calm, poverty with prosperity, hope and ambition from almost impossible odds. Then who could do it ?
It's rumored that Alan Blake got the ball rolling with Matt Cayman, Will Fence, and Martha Presley. They agreed they would need loyalists from all sectors, banking & investment, the military, successful

entrepreneurs, the clergy, a small contingent of
elected officials, the press and social media, and
maybe even an ex President.

They agreed the goal was to restore sanity, order,
and calm to American cities and the suburbs. The
country was on the brink of becoming Venezuela
overnight.

Chapter 2 – Creating the founding members

In addition to everything I have been able to read
plus stories from Grandpa, my Dad when he is
willing to talk about it, which is not very often,
and eaves dropping every time I hear the
discussion come up, I have been able to sort the
rumor from reality about the Agency's origins.
The initial 4 or 5 members created a list of the
knowledge, Influence, and command that they
would need to carry out plans. Invitees to the
board would be vetted and only told part of the
Agency's goals and mission for fear that the whole
plan would get leaked. They didn't discuss initially
the soft coup, the take over of the government, or
the take over of the monetary system and treasury.
Also not discussed was the command of the
military and local police, FBI, CIA, and all other
law enforcement and intelligence. Information
that they planned to severe ties with China 100%.
That they would ultimately control where and how
citizens lived, worked, vacationed, spoke and

wrote about issues, in essence abolishing the first amendment. At minimum a temporary interruption of the first amendment. and a mass collection of all firearms and explosives.

Each of these details would be revealed as close to the actual event as possible and still facilitate a successful implementation.

New members accepted to the board would be removed or be allowed to leave if at any time they came into disagreement with the majority of the board. They would be clearly threatened that revealing anything about the Agency and their plans would result in terrible repercussions to them and their families.

The boards originators and subsequent directors had pledged most of their assets to the goals of the Agency. They had upwards of 300 billion dollars to start their implementations.

The real key will be getting dedicated and like minded top Military leaders to enforce the soft coup. General Sanderson was the current Joint Chief of Staff. It was well known that he thought Biden was a bumbling fool, proved he had no decision making skills, left all the critical stuff up to his advisers, and had failed the American people and our allies around the world. The General had remained just enough of a YES man that replacing him would only risk getting someone in the position that might not switch loyalties to the Agency. General Sanderson was contacted by retired Colonel Odem North, knew him very well, about meeting secretly with Blake, Presley, Cayman, and Fence. They would meet on Blake's 1800 acre ranch in Idaho in July of 2023. Blake had been building an infrastructure with a bunker and compound already for a year and a half.

It has meeting rooms, living quarters, the most sophisticated electronics and communication to the outside world, dedicated satellites, food for up to two years, even a butcher shop and trout farm. It had pools, tennis courts, theater, and all the outdoor activities of a dude ranch. Deliveries were always at night and most work was done in the dark. Cameras, drones, motion detectors, and a crew of 30 retired special ops forces protected the compound.

General Sanderson planned a fishing trip for his vacation about 30 miles from the compound. The Agency's security detail would arrange to pick him up on a remote river on a Tuesday morning and move him 3 miles by ATV and then the other 26 miles by hummer into the compound.

At first Blake would meet in a closed session with Odem South attending to put the General at ease. Blake went as far as to say that he was one of many concerned citizens, successful business people, patriots, and politicians considering some form of participation in ending the violence, rioting and looting around the US as Biden continued to ignore the situation. It had gotten to the point that every night the various factions of anarchists would come out in about 5 to 8 major cities and burn businesses, wound and sometimes kill police, and destroy whole communities.

Yes, it was understood that these liberal mayors and governors had to request the Feds help but it had reached a point that they should have declared martial law and started incarcerating the perpetrators. They didn't say much else and gave the General a lot of room to respond.

He said that he was just buying his time till retirement in 1 ½ years but that he couldn't stand Biden and his Wok advisers. They had taken a great country and washed it down the tubes. The Afghanistan pullout was a human disaster. When he refused to even pick up a phone and call China when they invaded Taiwan last November, that was the icing on the cake. Australia and Japan pleaded for US involvement. They were ready to commit major troops and resources if the US would lead and Biden flatly turned them down. He went on to say that he had thought a lot about how to successfully move Biden out.
After lunch they reconvened in the secure conference room. Joining them now is Presley, Fence, Cayman. Harold Stone, Reverend Billy Johnson, Luc Allison, Miles Tuckerman, Ben Luciano, and Governor Ronnie Santorum. The general was informed that he was about to be

written in on a plan to remove Biden and his team. Now would be a good time to get up and walk out and pretend you were never here if you don't think you can hear any further details.
Or, "give us your solemn oath that if you decide not to participate that you withdraw quietly".

The General with no hesitation says he wants to hear more and he can be trusted that information will never leave this room. Odem South starts with thanking the General for those comments and says he was almost sure that the General would want to move to the next level when he hears some of the mission at hand. Alan Blake suggests that each member in attendance introduce themselves and a brief explanation of why they had joined the movement. One at a time they express their gratitude for being born American, the opportunities they were given, the joy of family and faith and freedom and how disgusted they were with the current climate and fear for the nation. Ben Luciano introduces himself as the little outcast kid from a suburban Connecticut neighborhood in the 1950's. He wasn't cool, had very few friends, but was very sure he would be successful in life. He learned business the hard way helping his Dad squeak out a living for the family with a local Bingo Parlor. There's no way he should have turned out to be a multi billionaire and a leading hospitality casino mogul. In any other country he would have become a good plumber or painter and lived a very modest life. He can't count the number of employees and friends he has mentored over the years, maybe 1 million. His kids, grand kids, and every generation thereafter will never worry about income. They could never squander his fortune. He owes it to his loyal friends and employees to be part of saving this great country and he has no fear of the consequences of being ratted out for taking part. General, please join us !

After every member has expressed their motivation for putting it all on the line for the success of the Agency the floor returns to Alan. He goes as far as he can at this point to reveal the basic plan without all the endgame details. He explains that the first priority is to regain calm and control of the streets. They plan to execute the takeover without firing one bullet. This is where the general comes in. Everything has to have the element of surprise. We need allegiance and utmost secrecy at the White House, the Pentagon, The Congress, The Supreme Court, and down to the Governor's level.
Blake goes on the explain the announcement to the American people on launch day. The Agency at the given time will announce it's existence and mission.
They will announce the temporary closer of all the branches of government and the agencies control of the military, FBI, CIA, all departments of the

federal government and cooperation from states and local municipalities. No longer will rioting, looting, or violent demonstrations we allowed. All offenders will be detained until facing trial without bail. The Executive, Congress, and Supreme court will be asked to take a vacation while calm can be restored to our nations cities. Business will continue as usual, no one obeying the laws should fear for anything. There are subsequent plans that will be announced to insure an orderly return to peace. This is not a coup or government takeover; it is a temporary measure. The very best minds and patriots of this union are behind this movement and have considered and planned for every contingency. Your safety, your rights, your personal property, and your freedoms are at the forefRonniet of our plans. We will be launching a website in the next several hours that will answer the majority of your concerns and questions regarding all continuing services of the Federal. State and local agencies, supports and programs. No interruptions of federal payments, medical facilities or approvals or licensing and regulation are anticipated. We are enforcing an immediate halt to immigration, both legal and illegal, and foreign entry with or without visas. These courtesies, not guaranteed under any international mandate or protocol, will resume as the authorities decide is appropriate.

Be assured that the movement and plan as

described has every intention of ending distension and violence immediately and the only way to do this is to separate the anarchists and criminals from roaming our neighborhoods and city streets and we will detain with no further rights or bails anyone disturbing the peace or plotting against this most urgent Marshall Law. Blake ends with, "of course this announcement will need review and perfection".

The general interrupts with a small discrete applause and contribution. "Perfect, I couldn't have said it better myself". He continues; We will need to get a stand down from myself and at least another Pentagon general; consider this done. I am personal friends with Chief of the National Guard General Bokanison. He hates Biden. We play golf together almost every week and take turns hosting dinner. I'll know exactly when to approach him. Not to put the horse before the cart, but, if we have the national guard we can direct each municipal police department and sheriffs office to follow a rules of engagement and control the streets and any counter attempt at the point of conflict. I'll expect updates and lets continue to use our mutual friend as a point of communication both ways, he can be trusted".

"With that all said I would just recommend that phone, text, and email communication be avoided, everything is being

monitored nowadays". Ladies and gentlemen, congratulations, thank you for your patriotism and best luck to all of us", raising his soda in a toast, "America will forever compare this to our Revolution against the British".

Chapter 3 – Trumps Return

Following the January 6th 2021 march on the capital Trump went mostly silent as the speaker of the house and company tried for the 3rd time to impeach the President. This time a President that was no longer in office. It failed, no evidence as usual. About early summer of 2021 regional state and congressional elections were taking place, some due to retirement or death. Sometimes requested and sometimes insisted on by Trump himself he began making appearances and rallies for these candidates. What was touted as GOP support rallies for these down ballot candidates were really, lets keep alive the Trump supporters and Make America Great Again. Trump could not announce plans to run in 2024 due to campaign laws but it was more than clear what his intentions were when he would comment "His work was not done yet". By the fall of 2021 he was holding almost one rally a month. People lined up for hours and days, 25,000, 35,000 and more. Thousands standing outside. He picked up where he left off. By the middle of 2022 you could see signs and bumper stickers everywhere for Trump. Still not announced he appeared regularly on his favorite Fox shows for an hour commenting on

Biden's multitude of F,,, ups.

Following Biden's almost non response to China's invasion of Taiwan in November of 2022, more independents and about 25% of the moderate democratic congress had abandoned the Democrat Socialist cause. Two congress people actually switching parties from democratic to the GOP. Republican potential candidate hopefuls like Ronnie Santorum, Kristi Noem, and Harold Stone had already declared that if Trump was seeking reelection they would not challenge him but throw their support to his camp.

By summer of 2023, 16 months before the general election Trump was getting up to 70% favorable polls. The Senate and House had already returned to Republican majorities in November of 2022. The far left, Antifa, BLM, the 1619 project, and especially the mainstream press were all freaking out. It looked like a Trump second term was a shoe-in. They continued to stir up conspiracy theories about Trumps previous sexual indiscretions, ties to foreign governments, accusing his family of peddling influence. They all blew up with deeper scrutiny and investigation. On the other hand Joe Biden was concretely tied to taking money from foreign entities through his now jailed son, Hunter. The press ignored the subject and Joe was getting off with no hearings, no censure, no impeachments, like it never

happened.
This further aggravated the conservative movement and straightened the GOP. The left continued to sow racial division wherever they could.

Chapter 4 - 2023-The year of crime

Dating back to the summer of 2019, liberal mayors and governess on the west coast, Chicago, and New York in particular allowed groups of thugs to attack buildings, police officers, the press, and innocent bystanders. Operating mostly at night, wearing dark cloths, and mostly masked, they used rocks, frozen water bottles, improvised fire bombs. They set anything they could find on fire, destroyed millions of dollars in equipment and police cars and attempted arson and murder on federal buildings. At another time and place these people would have been captured, tried, and convicted for 6 months up to 10 years. Instead Wok and weak local politicians and the new core of prosecutors and judges let the few captured out on no bond the same day. They were mostly on the street the next day creating the same havoc and injuries. Trump could not force the National Guard on these cities. Many, many, hard working small business owners lost everything. Some areas of Portland, LA, and Seattle became so frightening that the surviving businesses went under due to a lack of customers. Ad Covid and unchecked "legal" shoplifting and why would you every want to operate a business in these cities. Whether the owners were conservative, liberal, white, black made no difference. It didn't look like America of previous generations. Added to that, police were vilified. Thier hands were tied concerning apprehension and rules of engagement. There was no penalty for letting criminals escape.

Some were so emboldened that they resorted to assignation of police officers. Thousands of officers took early retirement or just out right quit. The police academies were empty. By the summer of 2021 local "wok" city council members realized they really screwed up defunding police and as crime statistics sky rocketed and people in very expensive cities like SF, Portland, Seattle, NY fled for Texas, Florida, Carolina s, where there was still some sanity. Rents and RE prices began to plummet in the Blue States. Tourists no longer frequented these cities and their attractions. Tourist industries also hit with Covid for almost 2 years now had a largely diminished audience to sell their menus and entertainments. Numerous businesses could not survive, even with free "no pay back" covid loans. No one could have written a better script for destroying industries that took decades to build up.
In the meanwhile, states with unwavering

conservative views and stricter "common sense"
law enforcement saw unprecedented growth.
Prices in Florida for real estate basically doubled.
Schools stayed open; people shopped and worked
responsibly with or without masks and shots,
criminals were captured and incarcerated,
protests were exactly that but not violent in any
way, local and state taxes were low or non
existent, and the best emerging large employers
were moving their headquarters to these business
friendly and "non wok" states.

With the obvious reelection of Trump coming
down the pike in little over a year Antifa, BLM, and
every other college age radical with no purpose in
life took it up a notch. They rioted nightly. Mostly
police stood by and watched for fear of a
perceived racial incident. Too many police were
being indicted or fired when the liberal courts
thought they used excessive force. They wouldn't
try in Orlando what they pulled in Seattle, LA, and
Portland. They would be jailed immediately.

In addition to the daily riots, looting became a
profitable pastime. Gucci bags, OTC medicines,
sneakers, would always show up on either craigs
list or even on corner sales tables following a
shoplifting blitz in these cities. Drugstores,
Boutiques, Grocery Stores and others began
closing doors in many neighborhoods. Mostly
effected were minorities and the poor who now
had few places to shop but also gave up treasured
jobs in the closures. Murder, Burglary, Assault,

Rape, Domestic Abuse, and rampant drug use sky rocketed. The homeless situation began to look like a Syrian refuge camp with feces and syringe needles everywhere. Local politicians were all talk and no action.

There was no single solution. But you don't ignore theft and other misdemeanors and expect to make progress on the bigger crimes. The Agency had many solutions which they would unveil in the months to come.

Chapter 5 The Agency's Agenda

It's now the Spring of 2024. The board of the Agency has already decided if Trump wins in November, although the cleanup from Biden's years will take a while, the Agency's intervention and radical seizure of the government will not be necessary. In the event that something went ary and he didn't win they would be prepared with their plans. Trump has already made clear his mandates and solutions to all the issues. Even the suburban soccer Mom's are ready to overlook the tweets and get their school control back, be able to visit a park without fear, and put the drug dealers away.

The Agency's agenda in chronological importance:
1. Eliminate or hinder the White Houses ability to communicate to the outside

2. Gain the allegiance of the National Guard, FBI and Intelligence agencies, then secure with confidence local law enforcement
3. The great Gun Grab
4. Establish a non hostile detention center for individuals and public officials resisting to the temporary takeover and changes to the law and order agenda
5. Establish federal (Agency) minimum penalties under national law for continued unrest or violence
6. Communicate to the citizenry the plans for law and order and install confidence of continued programs
7. Incorporate the Agency as a traded corporation with the backing of the national treasure and federal banks which would come under Agency control

Phase Two

1. Cancel all trade with China
2. Task force and fast track replacement of Chinese Imports with some new production coming under Agency control/ownership
3. Cancel all US debt (Bankruptcy) with special protection for American citizen bond holders
4. Cancel US dollar, redeem all currency for Value Credits and allow transfer of dollar instruments into Value Credits

5. All stock, equities and bonds revalued at 1 to 1 dollar to Value Credit
6. Bring home oversea 's troops and initiate training for returning troops, and other careers requiring employees
7. Review and change all entitlements to be work mandated for eligibility, the exception being permanently disabled and people that cannot carry out the simplest tasks
8. Reshape the federal agencies for efficiency, reduce military budget to reflect the isolationist strategy, and budget entitlements to meet the new lower demand and need
9. Institute a 5% flat tax and reduce IRS to a handful of employees
   Create a health care for all, allow for doctor care choice and limit services to illegal aliens
10. Close borders , no legal or illegal entry, deport any illegals for breaking the law; even misdemeanors and fraud or lying. Require all illegals to register or face deportation.
11. Revitalize home ownership by requiring all federal backed and private RE mortgages to be assumable subject to income qualification.

Ironically the far left, AOC and five, the radical left Senators and a good majority of the youth that was protesting capitalism the past decade will get most of their wishes. The Agency will underwrite day care in almost any business with 30 employees or more. Medicare and Medicaid continued in force with new Medicaid requirements for work. Clinics and safety net medical services were nationalized with regional out patient facilities including illegal aliens whose status had not been determined.

The new flat tax of 5% reduced the average middle class income tax liability by 10%, up to $10,000 a year in many cases, and the guaranteed 5% tax on gross sales for all businesses and investors increased the Federal collections by over ½ a trillion dollars a year. Ironically again, with the IRS all but gone completely, the corporations, hedge funds and other investment interests loved the new flat tax. It made planning and budgeting a whole knew foreseeable cost of doing business and decimated the in-house attorney and tax adviser staffs for many large companies. The anti gun group, got their wishes granted. The only thing the left could complain about was the strict workfare mandate but they had no further say in this. They didn't like the border being closed and knew the next step would be the slow deportation of illegals that did not assimilate into the American fabric or illegals committing crimes.

Phase two would not be discussed in open sessions of the Agency planning meetings for fear of distention and differences in opinion. The board had no rime to get stuck in any gridlock while phase 1 was being implemented. The long term reality that some of the constitution would be rewritten.

Some liberties like freedom of speech, freedom of the press, and gun ownership would have to be suspended for a short period. This announcement will be greeted with great criticism .

Chapter 6 – The 2024 Presidential Election

Inflation had hit levels never imagined. Groceries, especially meats and produce had gone up by 300% between the summer of 2021 and February of 2024. The new gasoline reality was $6.50 a gallon. Many Americans changed jobs because they could no longer afford to commute. Planning a 200 mile trip to see family took the same amount of financial planning that a trip on Southwest Airlines took just three years earlier. Big SUV's and Pickups sat on car lots collecting dust with the big reduction signs and window paint inviting you to negotiate a deal. Electric cars started to make a serious move into the Mattetplace until pictures of major backups at charging stations appeared on the evening news. Joe's transportation folks never quite planned for enough charging stations and would take 3 to 5 years to catch up. The nightly riots continued unchecked. The exodus to Florida and Texas reached the point that Ronnie

Santorum invented a lottery system to become eligible for Florida residency. You couldn't rent or purchase without the states permission. To enter the lottery you needed to have proof of a job or financial means, another words great wealth, to support yourself. This was tested in court and the state won every battle. Schools were open in Florida and Texas, Charter Schools flourished with the right to choose and the AC following the students,

Teachers unions were given a take it or leave it ultimatum when it came to parent intervention and curriculum scrutiny. The School Boards no longer called the shots, and parents were engaged through their PTA's to approve curriculum's. Florida and Texas grade school–ers were on average 1 ½ years ahead of their Blue State counterparts. Businesses flourished in southern red states. They attracted the finest and most qualified candidates for new openings and in some cases made large community financial contributions for the right to relocate from northern states. The Florida state coffers were full.

Following Biden's rejection to help in any way to stop the Chinese takeover of Taiwan, the U.S. had no credibility left in the world. Putin increased his influence in the eastern bloc. The Russians were now a financial powerhouse behind China. Iran got their nukes and now had all the mid east on pins and needles. North Korea continued to saber rattle. Probably Trumps personal visit to Kim in 2022 convinced the North Koreans to tone down the perceived threats. There was no more border patrol. Most of the veteran CBP officers resigned and enforcement was now up to each state, ranchers, and local militia to fight off the cartels. The border would actually move a mile or two every week as the states and locals would retreat and then put up an offensive move. Biden could not be found on the issue. The country was in a mess. Many said civil war was very close.

The Agency just about had everything in place. They knew it would be difficult to keep everything under wraps forever. A leak resulting in an investigation into the bunker in Idaho would eventually come about. Blake's security could hold off maybe a hundred militia or so but anything larger they would be forced to give in. Nobody on the board was looking forward to the day of the big launch and the hope was that Trump would win in November of 2024, start to turn things around, and the whole Agency takeover could be adverted.

Chapter 7 – Trump is assassinated

Throughout the spring and summer of 2024 Trump held rallies about every 10 days. He was convinced to keep the venues at 20,000 to 30,000 although he could have filled the largest 90,000 plus football stadiums. His team and the local police feared that the political environment was so heated that events could draw far right activists and have some outbursts of violence or confrontations with the traveling group of leftist troublemakers that of anti-Trumper,s. Talking points came real easy. Biden and Harris had screwed up everything they touched. Energy, Immigration, respect and strength on the International stage, repeated lies and hiding of the facts, crime rising to levels never seen, higher taxes, inflation at levels equal to Venezuela, controls and mandates on vaccinations. They attempted to force CRT into school curriculum. Attempts at packing the courts, admitting Puerto Rico and Guam to statehood to change the balance in the Senate. All this while clear evidence was exposed by the NY Post and freedom of information groups that Joe Biden received direct monies through Hunters bank accounts for monies transferred from Ukraine, Russia, and China. It was sometimes hard for Trump to pick the subjects for a 45 minute rally there were so many.

Trumps popularity had reached over 70% in the polls. You might as well have given him the keys to the White House before any general election. He loved the people. He loved giving back. It's estimated that he lost or gave back 50 million dollars during his presidency and the 4 years leading up to 2024. All of this to maintain the distancing of his financial world and not to give fodder to the press. In the fall of 2021 some news agencies both print and broadcast, began to play down the Trump conspiracy theories. They found ways to detract their 5 to 6 year unsubstantiated reporting of collusion, that Trump was dirty without lending any support. They reported more often about Biden's failures and how it was hurting Americans in every aspect of their lives. They began to be concerned about the divide and often violent clashed between hard left organizations and the Trump supporters. Trump wouldn't let up on the rallies. The crowds and demand for tickets just kept growing. He would only interview with Fox. The other "Fake News" had done so much harm to him and his family over the previous 10 years they deserved not one interview.

Trump was holding a rally in Sarasota on a Tuesday evening, August 18th 2024. He had been issued his Secret Service detail and always had his 6 to 10 private security with him.

The rally was at the Sarasota Bradenton International airport in a hanger that would hold about 15,000 people and they had monitors outside for another 10,000 plus. People had been camping for 3 days to get tickets. Metal detectors were not possible as every attendee had tents, coolers, little stoves, umbrellas, etc. As usual Trumps security team had recommended, even insisted that Donald go from his private plane directly to the stage, which he more or less agreed to. Upon arrival and exit from the stairwell of the plane there was a line of cheering and screaming supporters behind a barricade leading to the stage. Trump just intuitively moved to the barricade and began thumbs up, shaking hands, and an occasional selfee From about 3 rows back a 40 something male with a beard, shoved other attendees to the ground, pulled a revolver and got off 4 shots directly at Donald. The SS and body guards got the shooter immediately to the ground and covered up Trump from further possible harm. A Limo rushed in and within seconds was fleeing at full speed for a trauma center. One of the bullets hit Trumps Aorta and he died in transit to the trauma center. The nation was in shock. Memorials sprung up everywhere in the country. Rumors swirled about the shooter and conspiracies. Cameras on national news stations showed women, men and children in uncontrollable fits of tears and screaming.

The incident was already being compared to the assassination of JFK. Within 2 days the GOP filed lawsuits in Federal Court to extend the election till April 7, 2025 so they could have a new primary and select a candidate for President. The lower court agreed and the Supreme court upheld the ruling within a week. The country would have another 4 months of Biden they hadn't counted on. The executive board of the Agency convened. They had no idea who exactly would step forward for the GOP to run for President. Ronnie Santorum insisted that Florida needed him more than ever and he would stay out of the race. Conditions in the cities especially were real bad. Everyday and night there was now conservative and far right protests and rallies. These were met with conflict from Antifa, BLM and other far left groups after the sun set. There were clashes every day even with murders and police injured every night. While the Agency board were fairly confident a Republican would win in April, could the country wait that long. The US was on the brink of civil war if you wouldn't already describe it as exactly that. In addition just voting in a conservative does not deal with the continuing issues of the economy and US dollar falling by more than half and the continued inflation and lack of goods. Home building had ceased, builders could not afford the materials. Gas was over $8.00 a gallon and Biden still refused to open the oil spickets in the US. Simple groceries now comprised over half a families budget with more people turning to Macaroni and Cheese for their staple. That was even $4 a box. Vacations were long gone except for the rich. The auto industry had filed for bankruptcies and were making one quarter of the cars compared to 2018. Fireplaces were back in vogue as families often slept together in a single room at night for warmth. Small retailers had left main streets and big cities were boarded up with graffiti. Commercial RE funds were in the tank, even Home Depot and Lowes were hurting as the home improvement craze came to a halt. Change had to come about now. The board couldn't wait. Nothing congress could do would help at this point. The vote was unanimous by the Agency, pick the date, put the details together and go. Bill Fence got cold feet. He didn't like some of what he had heard about the temporary interruption of constitutional rights. He was asked to resign or be ousted by the board. He left willingly and told the board to keep his 30 billion contribution for the time being. He would take what he knew to the grave and say nothing, not even to his ex or his current girlfriend.

Chapter 8 – Our Hero's and Patriots are Devilified

Before George Floyd was murdered several other justified and unavoidable deaths of black men occurred and received national press. About every 2 to 3 months a new incident of a black youth or young male exhibiting violence or fleeing police was injured or tragically killed killed in the normal business of policing. Except for George Floyd the officers were cleared of any wrong doing. These often incited riots and extended periods of protest. Despite the fact that the majority of black deaths by gun fire are black on black crimes BLM and other activist groups persisted in creating a narrative of racism. The press ate this up and added to the fire. No one disagreed that additional training and vetting of police was necessary. The presses theory that there was seismic racism in our policing bodies gave some license to groups like BLM to promote the killing of police officers. And they did. Police deaths skyrocketed. Wok cities around the U.S. began defunding the police and cutting staffs. The results were predictable. Drastically increased crime especially in NYC, Chicago, Portland, Seattle, SF, and LA. After months of downsizing the protections of our first responders city councils were forced to begin refunding these departments. In the meanwhile rather than thanking these police, firefighters, EMT's the local politicians and often congress besmirched the whole first responder calling to duty. Police saw unprecedented departures through resignations, early retirements, and transfers to appreciative supportive communities.

Different jurisdictions changed the rules of engagement allowing law breakers to openly challenge the police authority and get away with all sorts of crimes. Judges and prosecutors turned felons back out on the street as quick as the police could arrest them. It was a no win situation for the police. Everyday they faced prosecution and their own personal freedom for doing the job we asked them to do.

In the fall of 2024 to add insult to injury, Biden wrote an executive order that any agency or private company receiving any federal funds would require employees to receive the Covid shots with no exceptions. IE; Even if they were immune, allergic, religious considerations etc. They were to be fired... Police, Firemen, EMT's, teachers, public workers, college coaches, pilots, flight attendants, and any private employer that every touched a government contract would comply or be fired.

Chapter 9 – Agency list expanded

Alan Blake – Internet Retail Giant
Martha Presley – Silicon Valley CEO, Philanthropist
Matt Cayman – Sports Franchise Owner, Business Mogul
William Fence – Retired Soft ware Inventor, Philanthropist
Conrad Priest – Ex Governor, Party Leader
Harold Stone – US Senator, Author
Reverend Billy Johnson – National Evangelist Leader
Miles Turkerman – Social Media Icon
Ben Lucky Luciano – Casino Mogul, Entrepreneur
Ronnie Santorum – US Governor, Party Leader
Odem South – Retired Colonel, Author, Military Strategist
General Sanderson –Joint Chief of Staff
Bobbie Winston– Board member Winston FoodMart
James Starr – CEO Starr Communications
Lucas Malkin – Former Financial adviser to

President
William Molasky – Former OMB Chief
Luc Allison – Owner Universe Tech Resources
General Bokanison – National Guard Commander
Red Jones – Majority Owner/CEO World Trans Delivery
Brandt Munchin– Global Assets Pres

Chapter 9 – Inflation, Stagnation

Grandpa Dale, my Mom's Dad, passed away when I was 15, in 2035. He told us stories about his college days. He went to University of Colorado in Boulder. Next to UC Berkeley the most liberal university in the country. They wouldn't even allow conservative clubs, rallies, or guest speakers onto campus. They protested everything under the sun. You didn't dare wear any Trump wardrobe items or engage in conservative talk, in or out of the classroom. Grandpa Dale studied political science and other liberal arts, not sure of what he wanted to do after graduating. In 2022 he would recount, the cost of everyday items and energy & gas had hit all time highs. A loaf of bread was $6 if you could find one. Regular gas was $8 a gallon in California and the cheap states closest to the refineries it was $7. Amazingly people had money. When the second round of the Delta Variant of Covid 19 struck at Christmas of 2021 the Dem's got another 1.5 billion dollar relief package through congress and every household got $2,000 per adult and $1,000 per child in one time payments. Federal unemployment extensions and add on's were made by executive order and would take months to be contested by the Republican party in the courts. Unemployment shot back up to 12%. Gridlock ensued in the production of goods, food, and imports.

A ocean container from the orient now cost 35,000 to move to the U.S. up from 3,000 just a little over a year ago. A container from Europe cost $22,000 to move. This didn't even free up the ports as American consumers continued to buy more out of fear of future supply and too much spare time and too much expendable income.

Americans already great consumers, replacing appliances and furniture years before other civilizations would. They had an insatiable appetite for home improvement and remodeling and there were no new cars to spend their money on. Why not spend your money on your single biggest investment, your home. Prices had doubled in most of the country since 2000. There was still such a demand for housing that Florida created a lottery system for new residents. You had to be drawn in a yearly lottery to buy a home, get a drivers license, change your address to Florida or receive benefits. Many Black Market schemes appeared. Lottery winners would be straw buyers for people willing to pay an extra

$50,000 to move to Florida.
Lines at the grocery stores began forming at 4 AM while clerks were stocking trucks from overnight deliveries. If you got in line at 6 am you wouldn't get in the store till after 8 am and all the meats, seafood, paper supplies, and produce would be just about gone. The packaged goods left on the shelves by 10 AM would be the ones no one wanted like Velveta Cheese and Vegetarian Spinach Pasta. A shopping trip that just 10 months ago would be $150 was now $600. The food pantries and last resort food banks were overwhelmed. People in their MB's and Audi's waited in lines for beans, rice, bread, and milk. Biden's energy policy had doubled the cost of production and getting goods to the Markets. Wages, for those that wanted or agreed to work had doubled. Restaurants, the few that had survived the last 2 years were paying $25 an hour to dishwashers and over $30 an hour to cooks. This was a windfall for the 2 million plus illegals he let in the country since 2020. They needed no training, it was legal to hire them under any circumstances. A family of 4 illegals working could pull down about $200,000 a year, get free medical, housing assistance, free public school and some college. A big change from the $1,000 a year they made on average just months ago in Central America and Africa. Americans getting $400 a week state unemployment and matching $400 in federal benefits, plus $300 per child tax

credit (mailed each month) and plenty of free medical clinics, food banks, food stamps, etc. would need to make over $70,000 in taxable income to come out the same. Why work?

The radical left in Congress never got their 5.5 trillion green deal spending spree of 2021. In some regards the left got some of their wishes fulfilled. Thanks to Covid Delta 2, they were able to mandate lock downs and restrictions, except places like Florida, Texas, South Dakota, and Alaska. They maneuvered and controlled much of the freedoms in the United States. They satisfied the whole group that wanted to stay home, smoke pot, and watch movies a temporary reprieve from actually having to work. They were still trying in smaller measures to kill fossil fuels altogether, slow new construction with cost inhibiting regulation, and free guaranteed income for all citizens and illegals. Most of the bills and issues were shot down, especially when most Americans woke up to the fact that the 2 million new illegals had a better standard of living then they had.

Grandpa Dale had seen the repeated ads for truck drivers. Local or Long Distance. Paid training. Signing bonuses of $5,000 to $10,000. Minimum $60,000 a year and up to $85,000 a year. Add to that all supply chains, bottlenecks were cured forever when the Agency took over in November 8th 2024 and added a .20 AC per carton weight bonus for truckers. That means if a long hauler had a 40,000 pound load going cross country they would get regular pay plus a 800 AC bonus for each trip ! The trucking schools and industry had all the drivers they needed. It wasn't impossible for a trucker to pull down 120,000 AC to 150,000 AC a year now. Grandpa Dale continued to drive trucks through his 40's and retired with about 1.2 million AC in savings. At the same time store shelf's were filling up again and the energy policy put in by the Agency reduced gasoline to a $2.60 a gallon average which offset the higher employee costs by three times.

Producers got parts on time, retailers maximized sales, panic buying and uncontrolled inflation gave way to price reductions and crazy sales by aggressive retailers, GDP increased to levels not seen since Donald Trumps 2019, and unemployment was reduced by 5% over a 6 month period. There was still 8 million jobs unfilled and the Agency had a plan for that.

Despite all the turmoil leading up to the 2024 Presidential election the stock Market remained steady, always with small corrections, and industry shifts, as producers and service organizations showed record profits for stockholders. The American investor, over 125 million portfolios, needed to put their money anywhere but the paltry 1.25% FDIC insured savings account. Still, the economic driver for most middle class Americans was the home equity they have achieved over the past decade or 15 years. It was either retirement savings or a piggy bank for everything under the sun. Towards the end of 2023 the fed reduced buying mortgage backed securities, the 10 year treasury started climbing at .25% a month, corporate borrowing was costing much more, and as a result home mortgage rates went to 3.75%, to 4.20%, and were at 5.5% by the end of 2023. With home prices just coming off all time highs demand for mortgages tanked. Home sales pulled back by 50% , realtors were scrambling for new professions, and if you had not got in the market at this point, most first time home buyers would be waiting awhile for interest rates to drop and inventory to increase.

Chapter 10 – Local Farmers Reap the Benefits

While the store shelves sat mostly half empty for the 4th quarter of 2021, all of 2022, and the first part of 2023, there was a good variety of foods available from street vendors. Makeshift produce stands and decorated tailFence of pickups stared showing up on every vacant corner lot that had space for cars to pull in and out. Small farms and even folks with big back yards were growing a full selection of fruits and vegetables. You could find beef jerky, small production organic lamb, fresh seafood, and every veggie imaginable. These little neighborhood, country farmer, hot spots, were frequented daily. Often the vendors were packing up by 10 AM completely sold out. Need an ear of corn ? $1.75 Thank you. Need a Melon ? $9.00 Thank You. How about a fresh snapper filet ? $22.00 a pound. Thank You.

These vendors were raking in a $1,000 a day. Attempts were made to license them, tax them, or drive them out of business. The customers and community went into an uproar at the thought of losing these last resort chances in some cases to buy food and the political control idiots backed off real quick.

Chapter 11 – Biden Retaliates against American Citizens

By January of 2024, 11 months before the general election, Trump had a 77% favor ability poll number to Bidens 28%. The DNC's convention was 3 months away and the common opinion is that Biden could never be reelected. Front runners in the Democratic Party were Elliot Park, a New Hampshire Senator and Paula Ashford, a 2000 primary candidate that placed about 5th in the primaries. Both were moderates. Biden was losing his grip on the socialist programs he had promised the radical left that wanted a socialist new society. Joe lost so BIG on all fronts it was embarrassing. He was humiliated by the press and the cable networks, as senile weak, afraid to speak, and everyone knew he didn't make any decisions. A previous defense secretary said that Joe had a 100% record for being wrong on foreign for 50 years. Joe was unmistakeably pissed off. For the most part he went into seclusion by the end of 2021 and left all communication up to his press secretary. Her response to this seclusion "Its the job of the press secretary to conduct communications for the White House and that's exactly what we are doing". Joe's agility, memory, and cognitive ability were past being a major concern. He was a poster child for memory or Alzheimer care and everyone knew it.

Both the DNC and GOP would not bring up Amendment 25 because that would put Kamala in charge and a brain dead Joe Biden was safer than the harm that Kamala could cause. She knew that this was also her last hurrah, that she would never be back in politics. On Biden's infrequent appearances or a unplanned encounter with the press he would get questions about his mental health, Hunters investigation and his uncovered involvement in the money scams. He would answer with the "Cmon Man", and are you some kind of junkie, and make headlines again for being the explosive guy he was. His handlers did all they could to shield him from the outside world.

To understand how Joe felt, how the loser syndrome worked at his physic, and what caused him to be so angry and retaliatory to the American people you need to look at his failures.

- Right off the bat, first day in office, he kills the Keystone pipeline, cancels drilling and fracking federal contracts and within weeks approves Russia's natural gas pipeline. Then when things get bad 10 months later he begs OPEC to up production and they turn him down. With gas at $5.00 a gallon and headed to $8.00 or more, heating bills growing at 50% plus and tens of thousands of laid off energy workers.
- Inflation out of control, largely due to transportation expenses, and shortages on store shelves for everyday goods and building materials in short supply he still refuses to reverse his decisions to kill the fossil fuel industry. Instead he doubles down under pressure from the left and writes a litany of executive orders his final 10 months in office to appease the greenies. This was a monster failure.
- He lost the battle for teaching CRT, Vaccine and Mask mandates in schools, and gender equity in the schools. Parents outraged when they were able to see all the curriculum from the COVID online schooling of 2019 and 2020 what their children were being taught, rose up in numbers to protest. Biden attempted to put them down by giving billions to the unions for legal battles and then sent the DOJ to label dissenting

parents as domestic terrorists. This all blew up in his face as a skirt toting high schooler entered a girls bathroom with permission for identity equity, and raped a 14 year old and then the school board tried to bury it. The same pert went on to do more assaults after being transferred. Parents of all colors no longer accepted the indoctrination that all white children arel guilty of racism at birth and all minorities are victims. 51

- With boys competing in girls sports taking scholarship and Olympic prospects away from girls was ultimately found to be down right unfair and illegal. Joe and his party lost on all of these fronts.

- Joe failed at getting people back to work. Unemployment went down in his first 8 months as President, but this was a given as lock downs were lifted a little at a time. The telling statistic was that 4.3 million people quit their jobs in September of 2021. The country had the lowest workforce participation in history. Service businesses, especially mom & pops that survived the pandemic, many with free tax payer loans, were now shutting their doors because they could not get employees. There were over 10 million available jobs in the fall of 2021. People that had been making up to $40,000 or more with dual unemployment benefits, welfare and food stamp handouts and rent abatement, found ways to get by without going back to work. All at the hands of Joe Biden and the Dem's, Thank you. Businesses had to compete against the governments free handouts. He killed the most important feature to the strength of the US economy, Americans work ethic and the drive to succeed against difficult odds in tough times. Like how we pulled together in WWII and following 911.

- On jobs Joe gets a big "F".
- Supply chain woes are closely related to Joe's unemployment debacle. Many truck drivers, warehouseman, longshoreman, and grocer clerks, that were either home bound due to a lack of childcare, just took time off and collected large benefits, took early retirement, or sought out more favorable working conditions, left the supply chain decimated. Joe's answer was to increase dock workers, truckers, and warehouseman shifts to 24/7. Great idea Joe but there weren't enough bodies to fill the needs. Furthermore you put restrictions on the drivers that worked, in conflict with your proposed increase in man hours to solve the problem. So the problem persisted with ships waiting up to 6 weeks to get unloaded at ports. The cost to business was in the billions. Not just from lost sales but a lack

of parts caused a ripple effect of layoffs on production lines, home builders needed to scale back, and doctors scrambled for everyday medications like penicillin. Another great GDP and job killer from the Dem's and Joe.

- The country reached a 77% vaccine rate by the fall of 2021. The CDC and NIH had said right from the beginning that at 75% vaccination level that herd immunity would take over.

- Most states had precipitous declines in cases, hospitalizations, and deaths by October of 2021. Especially states with no or laxted mandates like Florida, Texas, and South Dakota. Still, Joe insisted on national mandates for vaccines and masks. By using federal contracts as leverage, he threatened employers to get employees vaccinated with a drop dead date or fire them. This included private corporations, cities, and municipalities; they all received federal funds or contracts. The very people that worked 16 hour shifts, saving thousands of life's from COVID in 2019 and 2020 were now asked to leave their jobs, pensions, and security. States like Florida led the way in fighting back with lawsuits (17 states sued initially) and refused to comply. There was no exemption for people already with natural immunity, people with religious beliefs, people just afraid of the vaccine and willing to be tested on a regular basis. Southwest was the first major employer to reverse it's firing position and told Joe to go shove it. In the end strong political advocates of freedom, corporations with some moxie, and much bad press for the White House, Joe finally gave in on his vaccine or walk threats.

Another major disaster and far from being a uniter.

- Trump had created a plan for withdrawal from Afghanistan but it was condition based. The Taliban had to cease attacking Americans which they did, quit taking territory, which they did, sit down at the table with the Afgan government, which they did, and realize the US would keep Bahgram Air Base forever, which they understood. Biden changed the withdrawal date, made it known, did not insist on any conditions, and watched while the Taliban took 1 to 3 provinces every week. He made it easy for the Taliban to take over, they had a time schedule and the US plan. All, not some, but All Biden's military advisers told him to keep Bahgram Air Base for evacuation and future forward deployment. He went directly against them. He tried to micro manage the evacuation and as people close to him said; he had never made a

good Foreign Policy decision, he was always wrong. We brought 80,000 Afgannies out that were not qualified. Now they were on the USA entitlement payroll forever. He left behind Americans. American allies left behind, and, green card holders we promised security to for helping us during the war. He stabbed them in the back. They are being beaten and beheaded. He left behind 500 specially trained dogs that PETA pledged to find homes for.
We lost 13 young soldiers in an attack in Kabul. He staged retaliation drone attacks that killed citizens just for the optics. He blames everyone else. He was a killer. This was more than just a failure.

- The border had always been a problem. Trump made it a campaign and Presidency priority. He got the illegal crossings under control. His wall was 80% finished with the remaining fences sitting in place on the ground. Biden killed the wall project and the Americans paid for the installation, never completed, and the rusting metal anyway. He sent all the signals to illegals awaiting the call, now was the time to come. Within his first month the illegal crossings went up from 50,000 to 170,000. Small children were being left at the borders edge and sometimes dropped from 40 feet over the wall. Girls were being raped on their journey north and more and more corpses were showing up in the dessert. The summer heat didn't slow them down. The message was come.

- With border patrol busy in certain sectors cataloging the illegals, changing diapers, and being genuine humanitarians, the cartels picked their routes for fentynol, smuggling people, and guns, and other contraband. They got so brazen they would fire across the river at the US border patrol. About 40 CBP officers have died of Covid. The infection rate among the illegals is over 20%. They don't require testing or vetting for this and a laundry list of other infectious diseases, all while Biden will fire veteran officers, healthcare workers, and pilots not complying. With the border towns screaming for help the Biden administration flies or buses the illegals into major cities late at night with no warning to the states or local officials. The illegal crossings could reach 4–6 million by the time Biden is ejected. So much for employing Americans. This will bring down wages substantially for the liberal elites. Many won't work and the burden and stress on our schools, welfare and safety net programs, our hospitals, and food banks will be unsustainable. Americans in the middle and lower class will suffer the most.

- The Biden's and lefts socialistic welfare state agenda mostly failed. They failed on student loan debt forgiveness. They failed on amnesty. They failed on free day care. They failed on raising taxes by huge amounts. They failed on killing the filibuster. They failed on packing the court.
- Trump had North Korea scared to death to threaten the US. He had Iran on their knees. He had warned Russia not to invade any more of the eastern block, or else. He showed the world he wouldn't hesitate to use the might and technology of the American Military. He got the EU to pay billions more to Nato. He refused to fund the Chinese run WHO. Trump would have never let China walk into Taiwan and take over. He wasn't going to let us be ripped off by the Paris climate accord. We were doing better than anyone at reducing carbon emissions. China was paying their billions in new tariffs. Companies were returning production and corporate headquarters to the U.S. and large sums of corporate wealth returned to the U.S. Biden reversed all of this. We were the strongest the U.S. had almost ever been while we continued to return troops home and let our allies do more to defend themselves.

Before Trump would write a check for

nation building welfare he made sure the monies were needed and being properly spent. Many countries lost their handouts for being corrupt and in some cases promoting the demise of the U.S. So where Trump had the most common sense and successful foreign policy in place it's safe to say this is another Biden failure.

- Crime had risen in almost every major city with the biggest increases, up to 300%, in Democratic cities.
  They wanted to defund police.
  They discredited and humiliated the police; in some cases not just tying their hands when dealing with criminals but making it a liability just to go after a felony in progress. Retirements, departures to other jurisdictions, change of profession, layoffs by city councils, left the streets in chaos and open season for hardened crime down to shoplifting. Stores were closing up in liberal cities, leaving the poorest neighborhoods nowhere to shop. Chicago was a lost cause. No one could stop the lawlessness. Citizens were afraid to walk out their door. It's safe to say that Joe lost the war against crime.

- Drip, drip, drip. The DOJ investigation

continues into Hunter Biden's numerous payments in large sums from Ukraine, Russia, China, and other countries. It was obvious from Hunters emails that Joe was "The Big Guy" getting 10% of the deals for his role as Vice President. The NY post was the lead investigative paper on this matter. Information came out that as Hunter stuffed a bank account with these dubious funds both Hunter and Dad accessed the funds in the shared account.

Just like the "Durham Investigation" and all the Dem's seedy dealings in the 2016 election and then subsequently for 5 years during Trumps administration the report is likely to be buried for decades and everybody will get off Scott free. If anything this is one case that you can say Joe succeeded.

By late 2021 and into 2022 the liberal cable news networks, known as "fake news" and the three TV networks ABC, CBS, and NBC's ratings had tanked first 50% and then another 20% as polls showed that the American public said it could no longer trust the news or reporters. Along with the loss of revenues, investigative reporters missed big scoops, like Hunter Biden, the truth about the

border and Afghanistan, job losses due to stupid policy. Fox remained conservative but more important accurate. The heads of these mega news organizations reversed course and got the word out to news hosts and producers that if they wanted to keep their jobs they better start reporting the news accurately. Not to mention that the Nick Sandmann lawsuit cost CNN millions in defense and ultimately settled for Bias and inaccurate reporting, and defamation.

This pissed of Joe immensely. The liberal media that protected him all the way back to the basement in Delaware, twisted the facts on issues like the border, ignored photographs and stories about Afghanistan, the border, and his weak and failing memory. They had turned on him.

When they saw their ratings start to rebound they continued the "fair and balanced" campaign of reporting. Joe lost his big curtain to hide behind. He lost support from the moderate wing of the Democratic caucus. Especially with the 2022 mid terms candidates came right out and told him not to come near their state. How embarrassing!

When talk shows started making him the brunt of their jokes and historians said he would be remembered as the worst President in history he got vehement and plotted against his enemies. The far left of the party held him accountable for not getting through any of their socialist agenda. About his only supporters in Washington were

Kamala and Jill Biden. By the end of 2023 Joe began arriving at the White House on Monday afternoons and departing for Delaware Thursday midday. For the holidays in 2023 he took both Thanksgiving and Christmas weeks off. He quit taking meetings with foreign dignitaries. He wouldn't meet with House or Senate representatives and only called in his cabinet about once every 3 weeks. He never had anything to say. He would draw pictures on his note pad. The squad applied constant pressure to carry out their green agenda, On lookers and later memories by White House staff say he was always in a bad mood. He plotted ways to get back at his enemies, his own party, and the American people who had abandoned him.

He began to write a flurry of executive orders.

1. He ordered a moratorium on single family housing building permits. This was to favor multi family housing and reduce emissions. He threatened states and counties with holding back federal funds if they did not comply. Several home builders either closed their doors or came close to Bankruptcy.

2. He claimed the interstate Hiway system needed crutial repairs for safety reasons. He decided to pay for this by erecting exorbitant toll booths on the major interstate Hiways killing leisure travel and further hurting transportation, supply, and inflation.

3. He issued a national ban on gas driven landscape equipment. Mowers, blowers,

hedge trimmers, and chain saws, Companies like STHL were forced out of business and were stuck with millions in inventory.

4. He removed tariffs on imported batteries and electric cars just when the American industry had geared up their gas alternative fleets. There was absolutely no reason to do this except to maybe pay back favors to China for taking care of his family.

5. By executive order he directed HUD to offer 0% down home mortgages with subsidized rates to immigrant occupants with or without green cards.

6. He removed federal prison minimum terms for serious crimes giving judges latitude in sentencing.

Among other unexplainable executive orders these were all challenged in federal court. By the time they would make there way through appeals and to the Supreme Court the damage would be already done.

Chapter 12 – In all Fairness
Below find a list of the good accomplishments of the Biden Administration.

Chapter 13 – Don Jr. throws his hat in the ring

On a Tuesday evening of August 26, 2024 Don Trump Jr. agreed to an interview with Hannity. He was looking forward to it. Donald Trump was buried August 23rd. Don Jr. eulogized his father to open the interview. He wastes no time telling Sean Hannity that he has an important announcement and he his proud to share it on FOX and with Sean. "I am running for President in April". Moments of pause and gasping for air on the Hannity side. WOW gasps Hannity. He tells Hannity, " Sean, My Dad loved America and loved the American people. He felt it was his duty and considered it a privilege to bring all his knowledge and energy to the table for this great nation. He worked hard his whole life and the country paid him well. I embody the same principles and beliefs. We share the same acumen. He would be happy with my decision and very proud of me. He's looking down at us now with a big smile ear to ear. I'm looking forward to this change in my life and serving my country.
As one would imagine this plastered the front pages, the social media discussions, the TV news, and not just in the US but around the world. All the political pundits and experts came out. Most agreed that he would be a shoe in for the nomination and couldn't imagine a democratic candidate that could beat him in April.

The Agency agreed they had a little dilemma. Don Jr. would be considered a favorite son. The

American's would vote him in overwhelmingly and this would hurt the perception and downplay the goals of the Agency. Still with everything that Don Jr. could do to reverse the Biden disasters of the last 4 years there was still on big issue that would bring the U.S. to it's knees over the next decade. The national debt had reached 34 Trillion. The debt service, the interest alone, was getting unmanageable and the only way to pay the interest without taking the Greece formula,, would be to borrow the money to pay the interest. The Greece solution was to end all entitlements, safety nets, and cut Social Security and Medicare by half and default on public servant pensions. This would send the U.S. dollar into a free fall and cause national uprisings worse than anything seen to date. The Agency's plan included a default and canceling of 2/3 rds, about 28 trillion, of the national debt and a reset of the American currency. There would be with a short 2 to 3 year rebound on the international level and no measurable damage to the lifestyle or quality of life for the majority of Americans. The economy would expand quickly. They had to follow through in the next 30–45 days with the plan and one quick solution would be to support the elections in April and limit the power of the Presidency.

Don Jr. could be trusted with the exclusive responsibility of foreign policy while the Agency pushed forward their domestic agenda. It was voted on and settled.

Chapter 14 – Picking the Transformation date & the Board members roles

The plan for the takeover and the implementation in order of urgency and necessity had been outlined by the Agency. Time was of the essence now. September 14th was a Saturday. If the majority of the White House is at home, Joe will be in Delaware, Kamala; who knows and who really cares, the Secretary of the Defense Departments would be at home, most of the Pentagon, FBI, CIA, will be off and all the federal buildings, Treasury, OMB, and cabinet offices will be mostly empty.

The Agency agenda restated, which will be put into a public Press Release, to be distributed late evening September 14th, focuses on these goals.

Restore calm and peace in the cities and a return to order and normality in everyday lives

Close the southern border and regain American Sovereignty

Insure a good standard or living for all Americans

Maintain stability in the U.S. economy, insure jobs

and income for all, and protect the most vulnerable in our community from a lack of food, shelter, or medical attention.

For right now there is no discussion of the loss of personal freedoms, like some forms of freedom of speech, freedom to assemble, freedom of gun ownership.

James Starr, CEO Starr Communications
They hold the majority of contracts for the federal government for land line, secure data transfer, storage, cell phones, and redundancies is systems including the White House, Cabinet Offices, Treasury, Federal Bank, the OMB; the FBI and CIA, and the State Department. They also supply service to key managers, personal, and government cellular phones. With the oversight and direction of General Sanderson and General Bokanison, James Starr is writing protocol and algorithms with a handful of trusted programmers to block and disable communication for and individuals deemed a threat to the takeover and the offices of strategic importance like the FBI, CIA, Treasury, and OMB, and certain offices of the Pentagon.
The occasional Bruce Willis type hero can be expected to be hero's and try to destroy the mission but with no way to communicate or organize their, efforts will not likely spread from their local offices and meeting rooms.

The planned shut down will be 9 pm Saturday, September 14 and any access to reversing the shut downs will be protected by the National Guard.

Ben Luciano, Luciano Resorts CEO
Ben Luciano has dedicated the Luciano Resort Hotel as the first of dozens of detention centers on the Las Vegas strip. Although he is not concerned about the loss of revenue and physical transformation of his hotels, he knows that the Agency will pay to return them to their original beauty if he ever requested. Las Vegas has 150,000 guest rooms, about 85% of those on the strip. These rooms will house three levels of detainees; Minimum security non violent offenders or threats; Medium security; counter revolutionary activists without prior violent records; Maximum security; looters, arsonists, assault violators, and those who pose a repeat threat to the Agency. Any hardened criminals charged with murder, sexual crimes, assault, gun violence, will be referred back to the federal prison system with new protocols for parole and sentencing time.

Ben Luciano will call an emergency meeting for 8 AM Sunday morning September 15th at the Luciano Hotel. In attendance will be the CEO's and Presidents of MGM, Caesars Entertainment, Independent Hotel Casino owners, The Boyd

Group, Station Casinos, and any others that may be affected. Ben Luciano explains that he is a board member of the Agency and has all the authority to speak in their behalf. The Las Vegas strip will be temporarily owned and operated by the Agency under martial law and imminent domain. This is not up for negotiation. A perimeter fence is already under construction and I have enclosed a map of the strip boundary and hotels being affected. I can't guarantee when you will get your properties back but I expect it to be about 6-8 months down the road. As you have already seen last night and this morning from the press releases, this is not a coup, the Agency's goal is to restore calm and peace to American society and put down what would be an eventual civil war out of any control, which would have destroyed your businesses and fortunes. The Agency has almost unlimited financial resources. We will be paying you lease payments equal to your operating expense minus wages. We will employee every hotel and casino worker in food service, security, maintenance and housekeeping, supply chains, and even reposition administrative staffs if they wish to work.

The financial impact to Las Vegas will be minimal. We expect damages to your properties to be in the millions and will pay everything to return them to their original state when this is over. Security will be enforced with ID's, Retina, and Fingerprints for all individuals entering the fenced containment area. Each additional hotel facility will also have it's own fencing and security entries and exits. I will need some management help to get through this from several of you at this table. You know your properties, your employees, and resources the best, and you will be paid accordingly. These facilities will house the most low level offenders of disrupting the peace in our cities and neighborhoods around the country. They will be treated fair and with dignity. The threats of violence to employees will be minimal. Begin canceling any reservations, events, or conventions you may have booked. I will have more information in the coming days and look forward to your cooperation and participation in this once in a lifetime event. While the hotels and facilities are being retrofitted for our new guests we will be housing many arriving detainees at the Allegiant Stadium. McCarren airport has been taken over by the Agency and flights are being monitored and limited. World Trans will be furnishings transportation for arriving and departing detainees and also critical security details and supplies.

Roads in and out of Las Vegas will be monitored and screened by a detail of the Agency and National Guard. Lastly, my friends, it was all coming to an end. America as we know it. Within another month we would be Venezuela on steroids. We will owe a debt of gratitude to the Agency and their members who have put it all on the line to help save this great nation. Thank You

Ronnie Santorum Governor of Florida; William
Fence Former VP
Ronnie Santorum had become Americas Governor.
Florida had the best unemployment rate, a
booming economy, the best weather, and
standard of life in the U.S. The least amount of
petty and violent crime, great education, and the
ultimate in freedoms and choice. He was
respected and like by most of the Governors.
Former VP William Fence had equal admiration
and close personal ties to most of the Governors
from his years as VP. To a great extent jobless
since the Biden takeover, and an early member of
the Agency, he worked closely with Alan Blake and
other members planning the takeover and
planning the financial goals on the Agency agenda.
He had updated contact information; phones, text
access, emails, and immediate subordinates for all
the Governors. Santorum and Fence set up a
secret office location in Florida for their activities
with barely one staff member each
to carry out their primary goal. Florida was the
safest haven for their activity as Santorum could
guarantee protection and security and not raise
any eyebrows as he needed to visit the facility,
which was a converted beach condo.
The two had established a communication
fortress that would allow them to communicate
with one Governor, a group of Governors or all 50

at any one time. Their prepared presentation which would be attended by probably all 50 Governors was fine tuned for months. They insured the Governors that this was not a coup, but a temporary measure of unknown duration to return the country to lawful order, peace, and safety. That some extreme measures were necessary like Martial Law. That the Agency had all the backing and strength they needed of the National Guard and military. That the branches had been given a stand down and that all federal law enforcement agencies; IE FBI and CIA and been immobilized. The secret service was left untouched. They, the American people, would need the co-operation of the Governor's to achieve normality and peace. We are asking every state and municipality to comply with the orders of curfew, no assembly, and the immediate detention of any violators and trouble makers. They describe the resort like detention facilities in Las Vegas and the contract with World Trans to transport detainees, thus lessening the burden on city, county, and state law enforcement. The border was being closed for good. Air travel from overseas is temporarily being limited.

Otherwise it should be business as usual; Go to work, expect the Agency to continue federal payments, go to school, church, community activities, and enjoy the new peace and ability to walkout of your home. Thank You and we have given you a preliminary list of contacts for people you need to address questions to. As we will be adding and eliminating Federal employees and offices in the next several weeks be sure to refresh your contacts on a daily basis.

Harold Stone – So. Carolina Senator
Harold Stone has been an outspoken supporter of the Trump Agenda since losing to him in the primary in 2015. He was an early sign up to the Agency board and can offer numerous vital facts about the way congress and the White House operate. He also has many contacts and friends in the Pentagon. Harold will be tasked with informing congress of the Agency, the agenda and congress's future for the near term. No one is as blunt and honest about his feelings as Senator Stone. He was perfect for this role. At 10 pm Saturday night the 14th, one hour after the Agency released their initial press release Harold reached out to all house and senate members with the following release.
"I am your congressional contact for the Agency and all their affairs. This is not a coup. It has been necessary to invoke Martial Law while Congress and the White House have done nothing to thwart the destruction on America as it is sliding into a civil war. The Agency is backed by all sectors of the political spectrum and security forces. This is a non violent takeover that will last until calm and law & order return to our American cities. The Agency is staffed with some of the most brilliant,

successful, and patriotic minds in the world. Congress had their chance to bring unity to the country and quite frankly you fucked up. I recommend you take a long vacation or some time off. The capital is open but communications are poor and regardless of what emergency action you might choose to invoke, no one is listening to you.

Reverend Billy Johnson National Evangelist Pastor Reverend Johnson represents a broad spectrum of the American practicing faithful. Reverend Johnson will make numerous appearances on TV and Radio; specifically on Fox where is a frequent guest contributor. He will assure the audiences that he is close to the Agency founders and that their motives are the most genuinely sacrificial of their time. They have contributed funds to restore the USA to it's glory and insure the safety of it's citizens and ultimately bring a new level of economic freedom and justice for all.

Miles Tuckerman –Social Media Icon
Completely surprised was the board of the Agency to learn that Mr. Tuckerman was deep down a conservative and supported the establishment and constitution. He never purported to be a liberal, he was just labeled that way. Like the other successful entrepreneurs on the board he saw the end of an astonishing period of growth, democratic freedom, and business friendly

landscape coming to an end. He could lose 90% of his wealth and still live like a king. He had a big gratitude that he lived in a country that would allow for the invention and growth of an idea, like Our Space. Even more urgently his employees were his family. He needed to protect their future, their families, and their income. He insists that his company has never been intentionally biased or proven to be in court or other investigations. This will be the first time. He knows that the public opinion in the first 72 hours will be paramount to cooperation with the Agency. Our Space will reach over 100 million users with possibly 500 million postings. He has already written algorithms to censor out any negative posts concerning the Agency and Martial Law. He knows he will take immense heat for this at the end of the day but doesn't care at this point in his life.

General Sanderson Joint Chief, General Bokanison Commanding General of the National Guard, and Retired Colonel Odem South
Together these gentlemen know every top brass officer in the United States military. A non violent takeover of the security of this country has never been tested. There is no game plan to avert such an action. The element of surprise is the greatest thing going for the Agency. Cutting off communications to those that might try to snuff the plan out was their biggest weapon. General Sanderson will order a "Stand Down" of all

branches. He will offer his knowledge and support for the Martial Law and insure Americans that the White House, Congress, and the Supreme Court are fully protected and sacrosanct. This is really an effort to assist states, cities, and municipalities to get control of the violence, crime, and rioting; and bring a return to safety and normalcy. General Bokanison has ordered an emergency call up of the Guard and distributed orders and details to regional Generals and Colonels. They explicitly have insisted that there be no shots fired. Alan Blake has been secretly purchasing and concealing over 200,000 Byrna pepper and gas firing pistols which will be distributed with other pepper pellet guns and laser guns to the National Guard and local police departments. The board members and the Generals are confident that they will fill up the Las Vegas rooms with protestors, rioters, looters, and many counter insurgency threats from the military and political wings. Most will have comfortable accommodations and amenities while the Agency is solidifying it's control.

Martha Presley Retired EAS CEO & Presidential Candidate and Matt Cayman Entrepreneur and founding Agency board member

Both Presley and Cayman have run big companies with multiple divisions and thousands of employees. The Agency plan calls for firing of all

Federal Employees and rehiring with new vetting. As a team, no two better executives to direct this mission. They will need to first hire or put in place a large HR team with clear direction of the perfect employee, qualifications necessary. With today's allowable environment of background checks using email, facebook. twitter and other social programs, candidates will be investigated to discredit or not hire biased individuals. Through extensive discussions with Malkin, Molasky, Harold Stone, and with Alan Blake in attendance; it is decided that many wasteful departments, redundant functions, outdated bureaus are being eliminated. Up to 40% of the current federal budget for employees internally and the facilities to house those employees will be eliminated. Added to that the armed services will become a 75% U.S. based force with all our troop withdrawals and a 350 billion dollar savings to the budget. By the end of the first year the Agency will be a cash positive organization while expanding services and lowering taxes.

Bobbie Winston – Winston Foodmart Board Member & Alan Blake Retired CEO Sahara Inc & Philanthropist

The Agency will offer a 100% employment guarantee to Americans. The Agency itself will be the largest employer in the world. In addition to managing all federal employees and the military and with the redeployment of the military into the private sector, the Agency will run most of the banking, offer additional security to states, cities, and municipalities, operate the detention centers, and open businesses to full fill supply chains, especially those eliminated in the China embargo. They will open job training facilities throughout the country and also prisons and detention centers. They will open schools and colleges regionally. They will operate medical facilities for the under served and lower income Americans. They will operate safety net kitchens and cafeterias. They will offer Agency run day care centers for working parents. The Agency will have more jobs to fill than available applicants. The USA will become a workfare state.

Only those permanently disabled, hospitalized, mentally ill, or some other overwhelming exception will be allowed to not work.

Based on the Value Credit system, if a person decides not to work and has no exemption they will not receive any Value Credits from the Agency and will be on their own to seek shelter, food, and necessities,

Luc Allison – Universe Tech Resources

Mr. Allison joined the Agency late in the game, early 2024. After careful vetting and seeing that he possessed the same attributes as the current members; Money was not an issue for him. He had an endearing loyalty to a country that gave him every opportunity, a fear and loyalty for the security of his staffs future, and an urgency to make a difference in a declining country that he loved. Between himself and his genius staff of programmers and project managers he will write the programs that will be the basis for all Agency software. Agency board operations, command charts, tasking by the board members, reporting formats, and most importantly the budgeting process for Malkin and Molasky to paint a clear picture of the resources to the Agency (revenues) and new projected expenses by quarter and by year, and a 5 year forecast. The Agency will be issuing stock for a variety of expenses and the redemption of allowable large sums of federal debt. They will also be selling stock on the existing exchanges and expect the value to be a favorite investment for large institutions and small investors. They will follow the same reporting rules as any other corporation.

Red Jones CEO Wold Trans Delivery

Red Jones is a long time friend of Matt Cayman. They talk at least twice a month; usually politics and business. Anytime they are within a couple hundred miles of crossing paths it becomes a dinner engagement and an evening of deep discussion. One recent call when Red was showing his disgust for the violence and rioting and the inept response by Biden, Matt let slip, everything will be OK real soon. I can't say more. Knowing that Matt knew something Red kept digging. Before the conversation was over Matt invited Red to meet him at his earliest convenience. Matt did the whole "what I am going to tell you doesn't leave this room" and at some point you sign on or declare not interested and we never had this discussion."

Matt simply tells Red that there is a movement and plan that will succeed at taking control of the lawlessness and it goes much deeper.

Red begs to be let in and swears he will bring all his clout and money to bear. Matt gives him just a little more detail and informs him that he would have to be cleared by the board. Within a week the board gives a green light for Alan Blake to interview him. Red Jones uses a fishing trip as his M.O. and meets up with a horse packing Alan and Matt on a creek about 3 miles from the bunker. They greet on the river and head into the woods for a discussion. Before Blake can end the point he was making Mr. Smith is begging to be included. He insists he wasn't really looking to take a fishing trip. He pledges 50 planes on a moments notice to pickup supplies and personnel and fly them anywhere in the country. With Blake looking at Cayman for confirmation, Cayman nods his head and Red Jones is in.

Brandt Munchin – Global Assets President

Long time confidant of Alan Blake and an early supporter of the movement, Brandt preferred to stay in the background and has only met by secure teleconference with the board. He has never seen the bunker. Brian has been forced to close several branches in big cities in minority and poverty neighborhoods due to vandalism, looting and bank robberies. The cost of private security makes it unfeasible to do business as well. Now, he has seen a major uptick in defaults from his medium and small business customers. They had loosened their lending requirements back in 2017 and 2018 as the Trump economy set records for wealth and success in the creation of start ups and existing businesses. They were one of Americas largest SBA lenders.

First it was Covid in early 2020, then the lock downs that same year. The Covid relief bills and funding only reached about 30% of the businesses. Then the Delta variant in 2021 hit with no new funding for businesses. Many businesses were forced to close by liberal run states and cities. Especially hard hit was the hospitality businesses and food service. Then came Biden's extended unemployment which took millions of workers out of the work place with a large majority never wishing to return, so many of the surviving businesses had to scale back hours and service to levels that were unsustainable. He calculated that the SBA would never have enough funds to cover

all the defaults. The last straw was the supply chain debacle. By the end of 2021 Biden had thrown gas on the fire by mandating vaccines which resulted in hundred of thousands of warehouseman and truckers walking off the job or being fired. Now his small business customers couldn't even get resupplied to stay open.
If they weren't being burned out they were being forced out of business by the Biden administration. Brian understood the necessity to reset the American monetary system. He agreed with Blake, Malkin, and Molasky that this could not be a half heart-ed effort. The U.S. would need to default on it's 34 trillion dollar debt while protecting American citizen holders of the debt. A new currency, the VC, (Value Credit) would replace the dollar and be controlled by the Agency and backed by the Agency Federal Bank.
Brandt will be the lead in working with all national and regional banks, credit unions, and other financial institutions in the transformation of the currency. Agreed that the markets, DOW, Nasdaq, would remain in tack and Visa, Mastercard, Discover and other credit suppliers would be business as usual only lending and taking payment with VC's.

Chapter 15 – The denigration of our First Responders
Long before Freddie Gray (Baltimore) and George Floyd (Minneapolis) there was a small but

concerted effort to demoralize police enforcement, encourage harm and killing of police, and defund police departments. This movement attracted a lot of press and used the streets and freedom of speech to advance their goals. There was some bad eggs in every department but the majority of law enforcement were normal family guys and Moms just wanting to keep the public safe. The police before now were respected, looked up to, thanked, and even feared. Whats the first emotion when you see a red light in your rear view mirror? A moment of fear and anticipation of an outcome. Police were no longer feared. In NYC they were pelted with water, harmful objects, police cars demolished, and excessive bad language, all in plain daylight without consequences. Police in cities like Portland, Seattle, San Francisco were ordered to stand down when under attack. By 2021 prosecutors quit charging for theft, assaults, burglary, and many other crimes. DA's were freeing prisoners by the thousands claiming Covid precautions, lack of space, and fair equity. First cities invoked no bail reforms and eventually a national movement was made to turn out offenders with no bail. Police got disgusted that the criminals they risked their safety for in apprehending were often freed the same day and most went on to repeat offend. NYC disbanded a under cover unit of 500 officers that had been keeping drug dealers and other felons in check and removing guns from neighborhoods.

Minneapolis, Seattle, LA, Portland, and Austin made wholesale reductions in budgets and officers. Disgusted and under paid police were exiting the profession in large scale retiring or just quitting. Departments could not get new recruits and police academies were near empty. Emergency calls were greeted with fend for yourself in several cities or response times were hours if not days. If things weren't bad enough, Joe Biden through executive order mandated vaccines for all public employees by the early winter of 2021 or get fired. As much as 30% of police, fire, nurse, doctors, administrators, teachers, and even private employees decided to be fired or quit losing everything including pensions. Even in the best of times this exodus of the most vital safety personnel and experts would change forever the safety and peace of mind that emergency services, protection, and quality of life provided. Gun sales soared.

Chapter 16 – The national division deepens

If not already divided by political philosophy, perceived racism, income levels, and opportunity, different areas of the U.S. started to look like different countries. While the bigger cities and liberal West Coast & East Coast metro plexes experienced uncontrolled crime the south and midwest and especially rural areas were enforcing all violations of the laws. Shoplifting, petty theft, jay walking, not wearing a seat belt, abuse, assault, DUI, in middle America were all treated with the severity warranted and nobody was being let go without bail. Judges and prosecutors were trying or plea bargaining all cases. Mayors and Governors of many areas warned of stiff enforcement of codes and placed restrictions on assembly and protests if a dangerous situation was at all possible.

Florida was one of the safest places in the world. Ronnie Santorum was offering $5,000 signing bonuses for trained law enforcement veterans wanting to get out of the ungrateful cities, and they were taking him up on it. You could still walk the streets of Miami, Orlando, and Tampa. Businesses didn't have to hire additional security and shooting up drugs on the streets was a crime. Families with the means were moving to Florida, Texas, the deep south, Tennessee and the Carolina's in droves. It really was like two worlds and the Americans stuck in their homes and jobs of NY, New Jersey, California, Oregon, Washington, and DC were getting quite jealous and resentful. Added to that with the tremendous supply chain crunch and short supply of everyday groceries, gasoline, and luxuries, these more conservative states were getting a larger lions share of the goods. This really infuriated Governors and citizens in the wok blue states.

The press did what they could to keep the division going. They ignored facts and lied just about everything. They had been proven wrong in their early conclusions of Ferguson, Baltimore, Kenosha, Duke La Crosse, Russian Collusion, the Atlanta bombing, and Nick Sandman, the High School Trump supporter. The latter cost them millions in defamation claims. Then the DOJ got caught lying about using the FBI to spy on Parents attending school board meetings. This was a Biden inspired directive. So much for being arms length from the Dept of Justice. Unbelievably some of the populace did not find this outrageous. The worse the White House and demographic party blundered the deeper the Biden supporters (Now 38%) dug in. To admit Biden's failures would be to admit that Trump got it right. So deep rooted was the Trump hatred by this group, they couldn't admit the failures of the Democrats.

Chapter 17 – The Pot Boils Over

Following the assassination of Donald Trump memorials sprung up everywhere. Mourners gathered in front of the White House, State Capitals, Church's were full, National Memorials, places Trump admired like Mount Rushmore. Biden refused to order the American flag to fly half mast. Trump supporters of all ages, colors, gender, and financial means gathered to hug, cry, and promise vengeance. Religious leaders begged for calm. With every Trump memorial gathering a group of BLM, Antifa, and left wing trouble makers showed up. By day three after Trumps death, before he was even buried, fights ensued between the factions. Washington D.C., New York City, Minneapolis, Portland, Seattle, Dallas, LA, Chicago, and even St Louis had nightly outbreaks of fighting, gun shots, and arson with little interference from the police. Police departments were told to stand down and the officers were only too happy to obey. The news couldn't even cover it all. In Baltimore a 16 year old Antifa rioter was killed when charging on a group of Trump supporters with a lite torch. In Milwaukee a black woman was accidentally run over by a car and killed when

an innocent passer by's car was assaulted by Antifa rioters.

This further inflamed the opposing factions and the major media started to make it all about race. White Trump supporters against minorities, especially blacks is how the press depicted it.

It had been almost 6 months since the whole supply chain of food and other necessities had broken down. Large chains like Kroeger, Albertsons, and Publix had manufacturer contracts that gave them first availability for everything from toilet paper, to cigarettes, to milk and meats. The smaller independents and ma&pa groceries and mini markets relied on certified grocers and collective member owned warehouse suppliers. They received the left overs and as a result when supplies were OK or manageable mostly white metropolitan areas like Phoenix, Salt Lake City, and Orlando, the minority and poverty areas experienced extreme shortages. Most of the national chains had pulled out of the most violent prone areas of East la, South Chicago, Oakland, Downtown Minneapolis, some parts of St Louis and Baltimore and areas in the east like Cleveland, Gary, and Cincinnati. Independent retailers on the periphery of the minority areas quit taking food stamps. This was clearly a racial target at the blacks and Hispanics that lived to a large extent on SNAP awards to discourage them from shopping in their establishments. Armed guards stood at the ready at these stores, liquor stores and any hard good stores like cellular phone stores. Thousands of families had to travel 12 to 25 miles just to find staples like milk, bread, and diapers. This further enraged the minorities that had already been convinced by the critical race theorists that racism was alive and well.

History shows that protests that get out of control result in group violence and once this starts the participants are less inhibited to join in. Often Mom's, church goers, youth, even homeless people feel more inclined to join in. Once the first piece of glass is broken in a store and there is no evidence of law enforcement many are emboldened to do what they would normally not engage in. The police forces which have been diminished by over 40% retirements, officers opting to leave the profession, and covid mandates are instructed not to stop looters. They have plenty to do with protecting the fire departments and EMT's forced into the rioting areas. Large liquor stores are emptied in less than 2 hours. It takes about 1 hour for a crowd to empty a Walgreens. They will work on a Walmart with a procession of getaway cars for a day only leaving behind some produce. These stores are closing forever.

By September 8, 2024 you can see the plumes of smoke rising from LA, Seattle, Portland, San Francisco, Chicago, NYC, Minneapolis, St Louis, Cleveland, and Washington D.C.

Joe Biden is doing nothing but a daily speech from the White House asking for calm. The police and first responders injuries and even deaths are mounting and most refuse to enter into the mix to try to stop anything. At least 60%–70% of the people in these communities are not participants in the violence and looting. Unfortunately no one is answering a 911 call for medical emergencies, fires, let alone theft. The gangs are now dividing up the spoils one block at a time, each getting full control of it's inhabitants block by block, creating rules and laws of the hood you dare not challenge. Alcoholism and drug use is going through the roof. In some areas like downtown Santa Monica and the Miracle Mile in Chicago Vigilantes, Militia loyal to the Conservative Movement & Trump, and even shop owners have armed themselves to the hilt. With not much in valuables to loot in the ghettos and minority areas caravans are organized to infiltrate these high profile shopping areas. Before the word can get out about the armed resistance several dozen looters are shot and about 8 die nationwide, mostly black. These are described by the major media as Klu Klux Klan type murders which just further inflamed the rioting. Unfortunately these are the exact areas that the Agency, General Bokanison, and General Sanderson are going to have to focus on first come the evening of September 14th and the morning of September 15th.

Chapter 18 – The New Day Arrives

Alan Blake and his immediate staff of board members and techies are hunkered down in the bunker on Friday night September 13th. They are getting hourly and more often reports from the two Generals, Red Jones, Ben Luciano, Tuckerman, William Fence, Harold Stone, and John Starr. Within the secure system all board members are updated in real time.
John Starr reports on the override programs, and call diversions have been tested for all targets and that any subjects identified by the Generals will not be receiving or sending calls, texts, emails or other transmissions after 8 pm Saturday night. General Bokanison advises that a schedule of regular weekend and two week duty training of guard forces he has arranged. Training operations

are just outside most of the major hot spots and before they are relieved of weekend duty Sunday night they will be called for regular duty and dispatched within 2 to 3 hours to the metropolitan cities of the most concern. This will be followed by a general call up with the mission of; gain control, disarm, detain, and remove to the designated airport for transportation.

Ben Luciano in a press release on Thursday September 12 announced a possible outbreak of legionnaires Disease in his hotel and was temporarily closing to clean all areas and evacuate the air systems as a precaution with the reopen date unknown. In the meanwhile he had contractors standing by to retrofit his two hotels to contain minimum security detainees and the fencing contractors already had materials and staffs on-site as part of the legionaries containment.

All Blake had to say was "Damn Genius". Mr. Luciano also reports that his own security staff had infiltrated both the stadium and convention center staffs and both these facilities will be a 10 minute take down by the Guard and available for as long as needed. Red Jones is reporting through his chief director of logistics that an unscheduled need by DHS for vaccine transportation is likely to occur over the weekend of September 13 moving forward to September 15th or 16th. His routing and scheduling staff will need to accommodate on short notice planes at the following departure locations, Seattle, Minneapolis, NYC,…….. all told about 60 aircraft in 17 major cities. This is something very normal and accustomed to as the weather changes routes, handling, and anticipated arrivals on a regular basis. No one is suspicious. He will just need Bokanison's team to secure McCarron airport and divert all incoming flights except World Trans flights.

Ronnie Santorum and William Fence report that their script and all direct communications to all Governors is in place for 9 pm Saturday night. They will be up all night in one-to-one conversations reassuring Governors of this unprecedented move, the necessity and the positive out come. And more importantly, how they need to call out their state Guards and ask them to join under the command of General Bokanison. Talk to their mayors and sheriff departments to join in controlling and apprehending rioters and looters. Enforce the Marshall Law being implemented and local curfews as needed. Release all violators to the National Guard for transportation to holding facilities in beautiful Las Vegas where they will be treated humanly and fairly while being vetted for further possible threats to the peace. Local jurisdictions will not be overwhelmed with incarcerations and business should continue as normal for the safety of the public. At the end of the day many new rights that should be afforded states, like education policy, zoning, and public land ownership, improvements, regulations, environmental jurisdiction, just to name a few will be returned or handed over to states to delegate as they see to local governing bodies.

Miles Tuckerman reports that, against his fondest beliefs, but out of emergency necessity, the programs are written to begin censoring any negative posts about the Agency, any conspiracy theories, and promote the positive comments to the top of relevancy. He will be having direct talks with Twitter, Google, and Snap Chat on Sunday morning to convince them to do the same until all the information can come out and be disseminated.

Harold Stone with the help of Senator Tom Graysmith has the coffee pot full and a small staff ready to answer emails. There is no way he can have direct conversations with 435 US representatives and 98 senators. He will save any conversations for Sunday afternoon and volunteer a secure zoom call. His main objective right now will be to emphasize that the movement had begun, the National Guard is already enforcing the Marshall Law, there is absolutely nothing a single representative or senator can do to change the progress of returning peace to the streets nor should they interfere. The Capital, White House, and Supreme Court are safe havens and open as usual. The President is safe in Delaware where he belongs, but late Monday or Tuesday they will have a detailed press release of how the Marshall

Law is proceeding and what changes to expect as it relates to their roles.

Chapter 19 – The Guard is deployed

General Bokanison forwards his orders to the Captains and Colonels conducting training in 8 locations which he has previously selected near the hot spots. Most of the enlistee's think they are going home at 6 pm before the new command comes down. They are told they will be allowed one call home at about 7:30 pm. They are instructed to remove all live ammo and store their weapons. They are issued Tazers and Byrna pellet pistols and a string of hand twist ties.
They are given a quick demonstration of the two weapons and then instructed in their mission. They are going to assist the local police in securing the rioting and looting in the city they are headed for. All assembly's of protestors and rioters will be commanded to disperse. Any remaining will be arrested. Your field commander will have 5 colors of spray paint. Detainees will be sprayed with a dot on both their pants and tops. Orange is for looting & theft. Green is for arson or attempted arson. Yellow is for resisting arrest. Blue is for assault; throwing objects etc. and Red is for failure to clear the streets as ordered. Your commander has a key code and we have supplied a pocket flash card for you as well. We will use as many of our troop carriers as needed to transport

detainees to the airport.

Get a good meal and bathroom stop because once we are on scene we are likely to be staying for awhile. Inform your families or significant others with your phone call, only one allowed, that your extended service is undetermined but may be several days.

From information that was gathered during the 2019 riots on the west coast, Minneapolis, and NYC, the same group of rioters come out every night. Once they are emboldened that the police are ineffective and the courts have no intention of prosecuting they feel safe re-offending. Fox, ABC, and CNN have been invited to bring a reporter and film crew on the first flights to Las Vegas to show the human treatment but the serious nature of not obeying the law.

General Sanderson has got a message delivered on all networks and the social platforms about the Marshall Law. Violators, assembly, rioting, looting, attacking officers and troops will be seriously punished. You will be leaving home for awhile. Please obey the instructions of the police and military on the streets, there will be no second warning. In the first 24 hours they apprehended about 300 people in 8 cities. Forty were released at the airport as they were caught in the middle of the event but had other business. 163 were charged with illegal assembly, 42 for looting, 25 for resisting arrest, 30 for assaulting an officer. In addition 238 more, that had been previously arrested, were released from local jails to federal jurisdiction for similar charges and to be transported to Las Vegas. This freed up the holding capabilities of the local police and sheriffs facilities for more detainees.

Every Governor applauded the move, the local police and sheriffs had agreed to cooperate 100% with the exception of San Francisco, Portland, and Chicago. The decision was to let those cities burn to the ground and let them come begging. When the news organization aired the scene at the Las Vegas coliseum and the holding rooms at the Luciano, they were told by the commander in charge and an Agency representative that detainees would see a court in about 2 weeks and that sentences would vary from two weeks to 2 years for the offenders depending on the severity of the crime. When that message got out the crowds diminished quickly.

Chapter 20 – The Biden Team Scrambles

At 1:30 AM on Sunday morning at Joe Biden's Delaware beach cottage the standing secret service chief is awakening President Biden to report the takeover. Joe scrambles out of bed and heads to a small communications office they installed just for such occasions. They are watching live feeds from crews of Fox and CNN already on the ground covering the riots. Police are handcuffing protesters and rioters and escorting them to National Guard Humvees.

Sir; " It appears the Guard is in some kind of exercise with the police and sheriffs". "I didn't authorize that" responds Joe. CNN is reporting a press release from an "Agency" saying that Marshall Law has been declared, this is not a coup, but the cessation of all protests, rioting, looting, arson, and civil unrest.

Get Sanderson on the phone. Sir "We can't reach him". "We have tried the secretary of the Army, the Navy, the Marines, none are answering, their phones ring busy".

General Sanderson has the four secretary's of defense, The Army, The Navy, The Marines, and the Coast Guard on a conference call. He claims he is charge and requests them to Stand Down. General Bokanison is running things on the ground. It's not a coup.

It's a last ditch effort to bring calm to the streets and he will take all responsibility.

Everything will return to normal once order is restored. He doesn't tell them their phones have been blocked from in coming calls. He explains a patriotic group of very well known and successful and powerful Americans has planned this event, he has vetted them well, and assures the Generals that at the end of the day the success of this mission will likely save this country from the ruins. The Generals each separately give their pledge of support and applaud Sanderson and his group for making this historic move.

Chapter 21 – The burning and looting stops

The major media outlets are reporting an eery calm in the cities rocked by violence the last 8 days. There are plenty signs of smoldering buildings, broken glass, burned out cars, trash everywhere, and electrical outages. But as of Tuesday morning Sept. 24th the streets, with the exception of normal commute traffic are relatively empty. Blake, Cayman, the Generals and much of the team are taking a victory lap. Some local jurisdictions are submitting extra inmates to the Agency for detention, hearings, and adjudication. The Las Vegas stadium now has about 1,500 detainees. Some are violent repeat offenders, some assault, armed robbery, and a couple of rapes. The Agency with Ben Luciano's recommendations is opening a higher security facility at the Las Vegas convention center. Today the Agency will release a new information and guidance to the American People

"We are pleased to report that a new era of peace and normality are returning to our streets. We will be continuing to detain and transport offenders to detention and relocation facilities and prosecute for crimes. Marshall Law has been lifted but curfews remain in many locations.
Check your local news or law enforcement web

site. Our policing agencies have increased staffing by over 20%. We are announcing an across the board wage increase for all first responders of 20% retroactive to last week and paid for by the Agency. This is over $12,000 a year for most officers. All jurisdictions are looking for recruits and if you previously retired, have law enforcement background, or were let go due to Covid or other mandates we would love to have you back. The police academies and fire training facilities are all open and accepting applications for trainees wanting to enter this noble career and many are offering signing bonuses.

It is our goal to maintain to our best ability your American born rights and the rights given you under the constitution. While we repair the damages done to our families, communities, churches, government, economy, and foreign policy we may limit some of these rights temporarily. We apologize for this but consider the best country in the world returning to it's glory versus what we have seen the last 4 years.

Our economy is a mess. Quite frankly you will not be surprised to hear that we were on the doorstep of Bankruptcy. The Treasury could no longer pay the interest on our debt and keep the lights on. Printing more money was not the right decision. We have at our sides at the Agency the brightest financial minds and proven policy implementers.

You will be hearing more but our goal to maintain every Americans wealth, and stop the bleeding of our jobs and money flowing overseas, The board of the Agency has enormous personal wealth and has pledged their resources to the Agency's goals. Combined with your hard work, ingenuity, and American spirit we will be better than ever. Within 4 months and already in progress, every American will be given a promise of work at good wages. The Agency will need many new partner/employees and will be creating and in some cases owning smaller and major industries to fulfill the demand previously sent overseas. No one will be without food. We have a pledge of over 100 neighborhood stores dedicated to serve our plighted communities whose focus will be healthy departments of produce, bakery, meat & seafood, and dairy, along with grocery necessities. These will be opening rapidly and will not offer, alcohol, tobacco, cards or flowers, and will have limited sundries. We have experts employed to resolve the supply chain issues that have plagued our country the past three years and these long term plans will never allow for this kind of disaster again.

We have been leaders and in some cases the kingpin of Democracy for many decades.
The days of foreign wars is over.
This has cost us trillions in treasury and unnecessary loss of life. Often we have left

confrontations with our heads hanging low in shame. We can no longer police the world or expect our way of life to be forced on societies with a much deeper history than ours. Plans are being made to return our troops and civilian contractors from most overseas deployments. South Korea, Germany and the EU, Japan, and other remote locations will be phased gradually into accepting their own defense strategies. We will welcome home over 200,000 of our brave hero's. Many will be deployed to our Southern border, many will be employed by our new national Peace Corps which will work in our homeland to insure safety and harmony, and many will be trained to work in the private sector or for the Agency.

Our border is closed. Literally. Troops are now assisting DHS and CBP. We will not be accepting either legal traditional immigrants or illegal immigrants until further notice. Illegal immigrants currently in detention will be sent back to Mexico or other countries. Illegal immigrants in our interior; about 5 million entrants the past 3 years and another 22 million already here, will be registered and vetted like they should have been originally. We expect more than half of these to be returned to their homelands.

Congress has been asked to take a session break. The Agency needs to write. Edit, and enforce existing and new laws unimpeded. The White House and Congress have been left untouched but will temporarily be obsolete. We anticipate having the Presidential election set for April to proceed.

We know you have a million questions. We will be transparent and timely in our communication and dissemination of information. For now we can only plead with you, your neighbors and family, your co-workers, and your local leaders, to participate in this historic day. The reunification of the American heart and dream, and the joy and security we can all take knowing that our families are secure, well fed, and both physically and spiritually at peace.

Chapter 22 – The Nation responds in exuberance

The social media sites are crammed. The TV networks are breaking ratings. Everyone is glued to their TV's, radios, while surfing the social media sites. Relatives and friends are jamming the cellular capabilities. Twitter went down for ½ an hour and some phone connections just give back a busy signal. People are talking to strangers in the stores, on elevators, on public transit, and many workplaces have screeched to a halt.
The political pundits and historians on the TV networks are speculating.
Who is the Agency? Who is in charge? Are they conservative or liberal? From their releases it's hard to tell; they talk about the temporary loss of

rights, they enforce the laws, and in the same breath they talk about food and wealth equity and safety nets. Whats their end game. Will Congress and the White House lose all their power? Are they really that strong and rich?

Everybody is begging for more information.

Some analysts are calling this the most unifying moment since Pearl Harbor or 9/11.

It's too early for real Poll numbers but analysts are suggesting that the Agency has been accepted with a 80%–85% approval.

Chapter 23 – The Biden Administration gives up

Joe Biden had just two months left in his Presidency, Six months if you count the April extension to the election that the Supreme Court approved. Nobody was going to win on the Democratic side. The assassination of Trump didn't help the Dems. The Trump faithfuls were even more outraged with the liberals and Wok left. Now with Don Jr. joining the race his numbers rocketed to over 80% overnight. According to people inside the White House Joe was fed up with the American people anyway. He called them all sorts of disparaging words. Losers, Junkies, Idiots, ungrateful of his 50 plus years of service, his intelligence. "They could have this office and shove it," he would say. He had a couple of debts to settle so he entered his insane mode of writing totally non constitutional executive orders just to try to hurt people. His own staff knew he had gone off the deep end. He didn't need the headache anymore. He had plenty of money. He was writing his memoirs which would bring him about 5 million in a book deal.

He ordered his Secret Service, FBI, CIA, DNI, and other intelligence agencies to Stand Down. Let these Agency idiots see if they can make all these different factions happy.

Chapter 24 – Biden concedes

With Joe Biden making an announcement that he was not going to put the country through some sort of civil war, he would not cooperate with the Agency but he would not order the might of the Federal intelligence and legal system, nor the military to seek them out and close their shop. He knew also that the establishment couldn't locate the Agency or the directors accept for General Sanderson & Bokanison; and they already had the military on their side. General Sanderson has requested that the Pentagon establishment keep their eyes on our adversaries and keep the playing field even with today's status. If every an enemy was looking for a time to attack militarily, electronically, or even terrorist activity, they would see this as a weak point in the history of the United States.

Chapter 25 – Trump Jr. is written in on the bigger

plans

Harold Stone, a Trump family friend and supporter, has arranged a meeting with candidate Donald Trump Junior in early October. Blake at this point is not so concerned about his identity being revealed. They are meeting in a remote hunting cabin Blake owns about 10 miles from the compound. Blake doesn't want to reveal the location or existence of the compound. In attendance are Alan, Martha, Matt Cayman, Harold, Lucas Malkin, and General Sanderson. Each board member starts by offering their condolences, some with a little extra story about their favorite Donald encounter and thanking Don Jr. for stepping forward. Martha Presley recalls the horse face moment with Don Jr. blushing and offering an apology.

"Don", Alan Blake starts. "Your going to win, you know it and we know it. The first phase of our mission is moving along with great success. You can see the results in LA, St Louis, Baltimore, and other cities. The public is all in support in bringing back sanity to our country. This is only part of what brought us together. There is a much bigger issue looming out there. The country is bankrupt. It is only a matter of a few months that we will not be able to pay the interest on the debt. Your a businessman. You know if we ran our businesses the way congress had run this nation into the ground we would not be where we are.

They are like children with a credit card in Disneyland. We have a plan to return this country to a place where we will be stronger financially than the next largest five, G20 nations. The first several weeks, months, up to one year will be a little ugly, we expect more push back, and it would be best if you were kept out of the fray for your future. Lucas Malkin taking over. We will default and cancel most of our 35 trillion in national debt. We have no choice. We will create as little harm as possible with U.S. investors. The dollar will cease to exist and a new VC, Value Credit, will replace it. The markets and equities will be left untouched. We will take over the Treasury and OMB and rewrite the federal budget. Most of our troops will be reunited to the U.S. and the military will be downsized to about half the current size with most being deployed either to the border or moved into the public sector and the new Peace Corp. The Agency will be a corporation unto itself. As we decouple from China the Agency will develop industries to replace the supply giving private industry the first right to fill the gaps. We will be able to operate on less than 1 ½ trillion dollars for all Federal functions and return many responsibilities to the states. We will have a 100% guaranteed workplace and workfare will replace all welfare, unemployment and entitlements. Within one year the average American will have a standard of living far better than anything in history. We will not touch the health markets for now but will operate a network of medical and health facilities and ensure everyone medical care. We will make illegals buy their citizenship. The Agency and the new VC, Value Credit will be actively traded and the Agency will be one of the largest employers and strongest stocks in the world. I could go on for days but I won't. These plans will take us well into the century and be a model for the rest of humanity. Trust me, we have planned and thought out everything very carefully.

Matt Cayman jumps in; We have a very, very, important role for you in all this. You are smart, very charismatic, and a great negotiator. We, the board, don't have a lot of experience in foreign diplomacy. One of the biggest changes to the Federal government will be the consolidation of responsibilities, the elimination of waste and duplication, no tolerance for fraud or laziness, and a HUGE reduction in administration expense at the federal level. This includes the State Department. You would be the best person to autonomously run our foreign affairs.

We will no longer be the welfare arm to the world. We will not be intervening into everyone's disputes and skirmishes. We still want to be influential in the area of peace and human rights and want as few enemies as possible. Our defense will be conducted by a small army of fat kids chewing bubblegum, drinking coke, and playing with joy sticks, manning our 2000 plus fleet of

drones. We will probably send the UN packing, certainly not partake in the climate accord ripoffs, but need to threaten Iran once in awhile to keep them in check. This would all be your responsibility with whatever resources you may need ! Lucas butts in; One other little thing I forgot to mention. In our initial spread sheeting the budget. You"ll like this. We eliminate the IRS for good and the whole country pays a 5% flat tax on gross sales or income with no surprises and the Agency still operates in the black building wealth for the stockholders and the American people. Don Jr. shakes his head and lets out a , WOW. That's a lot to digest. I'm liking what I hear but I need to mull this over and I am sure I will have many questions. Another words; you will want me to conduct all foreign policy and stay out of domestic policy ? Harold jumps in; That's about the scope of it, although you will play an advisory roll on all domestic policy.
Don asks. What about congress?
Alan reply's right away ! Who ?

Chapter 26 – All Calm on the Western Front

It's been eight weeks since the September 14th takeover. Bob Walton has just opened 10 of the regional neighborhood groceries and has six a week planned for the next 2 months, all in minority, impoverished, and especially burnt out shopping areas from the August and September

riots. They have enough security that no one will attempt looting let alone shoplifting. These stores are so popular people are traveling for miles from outside of these neighborhoods to shop. The prices are lower, the focus is natural and fresh, it's easy to find things, and customers are very safe to park and shop. About another 900 detainees have been moved to Las Vegas. Most are younger Marxist sympathizers but included in the mix are drug dealers, gun sellers, auto thief's, and some accused of using a firearm in the commission of a crime. Any murder, rape, or domestic violence cases are still being handled at the local level. The drug dealers and gun violators have a special place in the convention center and will be moved to a federal prison soon for an extended stay. There has been a measurable downturn in the gun violence in places like Chicago and Baltimore. The Agency has made it clear that gun and drug offenses will be dealt with swiftly, don't expect "no cash bail",
that's gone forever, don't expect any bail, and expect to be locked up for a long rime. On the border, in addition to NO new illegals sneaking past the 5,000 national guard, they project that not a drop of drugs has made it into the United States for three weeks. Underground drug details report that all the drugs, especially Fentyonl, have quadrupled in price, if you can find it. This simple supply and demand measurement shows you the supply line is drying up. Billboards in Mexico

advertise " ¿Necesita unas vacaciones de 10 años en Leavenworth? ¡Solo trae algunas drogas a América!, Need a 10 year vacation to Leavenworth, Bring some drugs to America.

The press, even the liberal MSNBC, CNN, and the three networks are applauding the work and success of the Agency. They think it is a liberal or Democratic party related group running the show. General Sanderson has created with Miles Cayman an initial flyer for the armed forces discussing career opportunities following their service. All of the military got a 5% raise just last week. Not very many enlistees or officers are interested in joining or supporting any attempt to unseat the Agency. The Agency now has what is believed 100% cooperation with local law enforcement across the country. They have never been so happy to be able to do their job again and they are being applauded and thanked by all citizens.

The Agency recruited about 100 retired special op's and Seals as their private security and emergency crew to put down any counter insurrections. The local police are handling the smaller urban and rural conspiracies. These violators are whisked off to Las Vegas.
These special agents will be instrumental in the swift take over of the Treasury, OMB, and the Federal Reserve Bank of NY.

Chapter 27 – Eight Representatives take a vacation

General Sanderson has been requested for a special meeting at the Pentagon on October 23, 2024. He assumes this will be an attempt to put him under arrest so he suggests an alternative location in the DC area which he will text 15 minutes before the meeting. He will be joined by about 20 of his men in black, the special ops corp of the Agency.

They meet in a Starbucks with plenty of on lookers for safety. No one would pull a gun in this environment. He also has escape plans out the back. A Colonel in charge of Pentagon security informs him that they have been in contact with a small group of US representatives and Senators who have requested a plan to overtake the Agency and put them out of business. At the direction of two, 3 star Generals, they have played along like they were interested. Now that it was time to pick a date and targets they are bringing the plan to General Sanderson.

The Colonel details the names of 6 US House of Representatives and 2 Senators, all democrats except for one. The next morning eight special ops teams of about 10 members each are waiting for the staffs of the eight congress people to arrive to work or they have already

been to the law makers homes at 4AM to offer them a ride to the airport. Their offices were closed and the employees told to go home. The law makers were whisked to Ronald Reagan airport where a Fedex flight was waiting for their arrival. Their cell phones were seized. In Las Vegas Ben Luciano has prepared eight luxury suites for his new quests. He is alerted 5 minutes before their arrival at the Luciano VIP entrance where he greets them with diplomatic protocols only afforded high rollers and celebrities.

They are given a tour of the Spa, the pool, the gourmet buffet, library, and another 5 choices for gourmet dining. He joins the bell hops in welcoming them to their suites and informs them that the house phones are just that, room service and house keeping, that they cannot access an outside line. They will be allowed one phone call to a loved one which will be monitored later in the day and he invites them to a special welcome dinner hosted by himself, Ben Luciano.

Harold Stone contacts the families of the eight detainees and assures them that the group is safe and enjoying themselves in a luxurious hotel with all the amenities. He releases a press announcement at the same time describing how the effort to dislodge the Agency was adverted and how the terribly mistaken law makers would not be seeing their families until at least the Spring of 2025.

This sends a message to all of congress, the White House, the courts, federal and civilian employees of the government and any dissenters that the Agency is completely in control and will not look favorably on attempts not to cooperate.

Chapter 28 – It's all about the money

The Agency has picked September 28th, a Sunday, to mobilize their team to take over the OMB of 17th street DC, the Treasury next to the White House, and the Federal Reserve at 33 Liberty St. NYC on Monday morning before workers arrive. They have a complete shakedown of the security in these buildings and it is really some out of date monitors, overweight police wannabees that flunked out of the police academies, that they need to address. They will be taken by surprise and held offsite at a distance till their security managers can retrieve them later in the day. Lucas Malkin will show at the Treasury at 6:30 AM with his group of men in black and about 5 propeller heads he has chosen and done some training with. His first call will be to Jerry Pope, head of the Federal Reserve, to announce his retirement, and tell him that the Agency will be looking for good candidates, he might send in his resume. The treasury has about 10 key employees that Lucas wants to retain that have knowledge that will expedite his goals. Martha Presley is on hand with a small team of HR specialists to make offers with raises and bonus's for their retention and to pledge allegiance to Mr. Malkin and the Agency. The rest of the employees are given a website to go view a large range of open positions with the Agency, job training programs, and offers for early retirement. The Agency has identified over 300,000 openings in it's initial forecasts.

Mr. Pope, Larry says with a long pause and a deep and loud infliction, "Instruct all your staffs, top to bottom, to cooperate with this transformation, including all subsidy branches of the Federal Bank Depository, or, explain we have openings in Las Vegas for sweepers and potato peelers that have guaranteed longevity, if you know what I mean.

The same scene ensues at the OMB. Earl Molasky knows the exact list of current employees he wants at his side. Many that he had groomed under the Trump administration. With his group of men in black and newly trained computer whizzes he takes over like he had never left for four years. Miles Cayman has a team of HR specialists that are offering similar bonus's and raises and vetting selected managers for permanent positions.

At the Federal Bank in New York the security is a little tighter. The Agency's front team has gained an insider with the Banks security detail and arranged for a bomb threat evacuation at 6:00 AM. Before most employees arrive for work. The NY Chief of Police is in the know and has directed precincts and patrols to take a hands off. The current President of Global Assets, Brandt Munchin, is joining Luc Allison from Universal Tech to greet the Banks CEO on arrival.

The bank President is informed of the takeover and the already occupied and new principals of the Treasury and OMB. They dial up Mr. Pope and wish him a good morning from NYC and open the speaker to the Federal Banks President, as Pope confirms it is all real and to cooperate fully.

Amazingly, since September 14th there has been a couple warning shots from live ammo in the air. Not one bullet fired or person shot during this whole takeover. The stun guns and pellet pistols came in very handy with crowd control in the beginning. No one wanted to test the black suited men in their dark sunglasses and their smoke window Suburbans. With much speed the passwords, pins, and other safeguards are in the hands of Lucas Malkin, Earl Molasky, and the Bunker in Idaho. The Agency has just pulled off a 250 billion heist without a gun or a hostage. Equally important, the 10 billion plus a day that flows into the Fed, IRS, Customs, and all other revenue streams of the US now flows directly to the Agency. And no one other than Earl Molaskey can write checks or authorize bank transfers without him or his trusted staffs approval.

Check reclamation is a recovery procedure used by the Bureau of the Fiscal Service (Fiscal Service) to obtain refunds (reclamations) from a presenting bank for paid Treasury checks.

Alan Blake and Lucas Malkin have determined over 300 billion in Payments that they intend to reclaim through this provision for interest paid on national debt, some stupid Biden pet projects like the Illegal alien payments of ½ million dollars per person, funds to the Taliban, and some other countries not deserving of the US taxpayers hard earned dollars. As well, just for fun they are going to bounce Biden's payroll checks as President.

Chapter 29 – The Agency's pocket book

The biggest challenge by far for the Agency will be rewriting the Federal budget and getting popular support as some pet projects and entitlements go away. As a general rule the most Liberal of all politicians are getting their dreams come true with a new Tax Code, equity in wealth and cost sharing, and many programs they had pushed for. The Agency cannot begin to revamp the bureaucratic costs, waste, and fraud until they have a handle on the income and net worth side of the government.

The Agency will be creating over 4 million jobs, not including the jobs created by the public sector, as it eliminates some departments and positions, transfers and opens others. The Agency will operate it's own portfolio of companies that to a large extent will fill supply that is being created from a decoupling with China.
The Agency net worth and income streams boil down to this

The Agency Board has dedicated 300 billion in

personal wealth
300 B
(This will be secured by Agency stock valued at $1
to 1 VC)

The federal reserve now in control of the Agency
holds *3.8 Trillion*

The Agency will generate *90 Billion* annually in
Tariffs
The new Tax Code will be 5% of Gross Income(no
deductions) 2 *Trillion* annually
Illegals will pay $100 per month per illegal for 12
years for citizenship *30 B*

Other Fees and Licenses, Leases *50 B* annualy

5.7 Trillion (FY 1)

The Agency will not be spending the 3.8 Trillion
held by the Federal Reserve. This just reflects a
total of cash available to the Agency if needed in
FY 1.

The actual revenue projected revenue (+or– 5%)
with the new flat tax of 5% is 2 Trillion AC.

In 2010 the Financial budget was 2.16 trillion, In
2000 the Financial Budget was 2.10 Trillion.
It grew to 3.86 Trillion by 2020. What happened
was Congress went drunk nuts with spending and

the interest liabilities got out of control along with stimulus spending, Covid relief, some natural disasters and a very generous check book with foreign nations got us in deeper. The Agency will keep a fiscal budget of 2 Trillion while increasing services greatly and reducing taxes to ordinary Americans by over 150%..

Chapter 30 – Workfare

For many decades the level of fraud and lack of adherence to entitlement laws had grown out of control. Recipients often aided by county and state workers found it increasingly easy to game the system for Section 8 housing, Food Stamps, Welfare payments, Child Tax credits and other programs designed as safety nets for the needy. Unemployment fraud reached 20 Billion dollars in California during the Covid pandemic, even with prison inmates getting checks in the mail.

The Agency was ditching all the programs and bringing them under one roof. To some extent their plans fulfilled another radical left dream of guaranteed income for all. The only thing the left had not planned for was that people might actually have to go to work. The Agency has a task force, a clearing house you might say, for employment openings throughout the country in the private industry but also the Agency itself, states, counties, and cities.

People with severe disabilities, like blindness, deaf, quadriplegic, serious mental illness or any other debilitating impairment that would keep them from answering a phone, using a keyboard, possibly driving a vehicle, may be exempt subject to an Agency audit and examination. Otherwise, "We have a job for you". Even for individuals with no formal education past grade school they had jobs in security, administration, customer service, driving school buses and transportation for seniors, cafeteria work, housekeeping, property maintenance, child supervision and day care work, and the list goes on.

Traditional unemployment no longer exists. With over 12 million unfilled positions, and the Agency adding new positions every month, there is no reason for 7 million people collecting unemployment. Even if people are in a career change and looking, they can work temporarily for the Agency.

The poverty level in 2022 was about 12,000 VC per year for a single person 22.000 VC for a family of 3. We know these statistics are always months or years behind. Example: As the Social Security Administration announced a 5.9% cost of living increase for 2022 in October of 2021, inflation numbers came out in November of 2021 of 6.2%. In essence this earased the total COLA increase being paid based on 2020 numbers before the first increase was ever paid on January of 2022. Another words, thank you for nothing. Housing costs vary greatly from state to state and county to county. So the Agency got real time cost of living statistics for all jurisdictions. If the Agency or a private employer, employed you at 15 VC per hour, which is about the minimum even in food service, at 40 hours you would get 2,400 VC per month, 28,800 VC a year. In real time in a California coastal town the minimum cost of living for a family of three was 35,000 VC per year. Your single parent income was 28,800 VC for the year. The Agency would then subsidize your income 6,200 VC a year or 516 VC per month. As soon as you have a subsidy award your VC card is blocked from purchasing alcohol or cigarettes. By using this formula the Agency will save about 50% of the current entitlements and welfare payments and eliminate fraud. A savings to the taxpayer of about 300 Billion VC a year. The Agency subsidy is all inclusive for any previous welfare, housing, food stamps, or other program. The plan was designed to be a single source safety net, elevating low income wage earners to a reasonable level, paying the way for permanently disable individuals, while forcing certain people off the couch to get back to work. If one cannot manage their income based on the Agency's award and formula then intervention is created to see where the money is going and any lack of responsibility of the recipient.

If you have three dependent children and we see from your VC card your spending 300 VC a month for nails and hair styling then someone from child welfare will be knocking at your door. If you are a deadbeat Dad, there's no courts, no Sheriffs, no garnishments. The moment funds hit your VC card they are gobbled up for your children.

This becomes another talking point for those that enjoyed gaming the welfare system. They should be thankful the Agency is not auditing backwards and collecting for awards that should have never been made.

Chapter 31 – The Silent Gun Grab

Like some other hot topics all you need to do is whisper Gun Control and many hundreds of thousands take to the social media sites and start waving NRA banners. The Supreme Court Steps and any other legal or illegal method of protest are full of pro 2nd amendment activists. Law Enforcement and Congress and Local Politicians have been trying for years to outlaw guns wherever they could, legal guns, illegal guns, black Mileset guns, guns sold on web sites and shows, and on, to reduce gun violence, especially with gangs.

The Agency has begun a policy campaign with

very crafty press releases and often buries hot topics in the text to let them drip, drip, drip, over time. The Agency doesn't have a face, except the Generals, Cayman, Malkin, and Molasky and everyone knows these are just soldiers. The Agency has no phone number, no tweeter account, no address.

In a Mid October press release the Agency implores the public to read this message, and probably twice.

" We are in the midst of declaring victory on crime and chaos. It's safe to go to work, school, shopping, or a walk in almost all communities. The revitalization of badly damaged neighborhoods during the unrest is on-going with many new great shopping and food supply choices, cleaned up public areas, removal of trash, freshly renovated schools and more.

This is very, very important. In order to restore sanity and bring prosperous growth to our families, especially in middle and low income areas, we had no other choice but to take control of the law and protection of the country. Equally important, the US economy was going down the tubes. There will be much discussion and information about this subject. Before our new President would have been sworn in, in April of next year, we would have been bankrupt. To go bankrupt without a plan would have left us worse

off than Venezuela. We would have been the least
desirable nation to live in, in the world. With your
money worth nothing, no supplies, no jobs,
surging crime, and probably revolution.
With every cure comes just a little pain. We ask
you to believe in us and give us your support
moving forward.
Here is a broad stroke of things you can expect in
the near future.

- We will inaugurate a new President in April
- We expect to be employing EVERY American
  within the next 6 months at great paying
  jobs
- The Agency itself will create and run several
  business models to bridge gaps in supply
  shortages
- A new currency will strengthen and save
  your net worth, your retirement funds etc.
- The equity and bond markets will continue
  to operate and thrive on any changes
- We will seek to reduce the amount of guns
  on the streets

(They don't mention this will be done by forced
buybacks, manufacturer and gun shop shutdowns
and eventual gun grabs)

- The face of congress will change

(They fail to mention that Congress will be closed
till further notice and the savings will be in the
billions)

- We are bringing our forces home to join the
  new domestic peace corp and honoring

them with education and jobs of their choice

- We are stream lining the Federal budget, adding efficiencies resulting in billions of tax dollar savings
- We are balancing the Federal budget, enhancing and making fraud proof safety nets while adding guaranteed medical care, education where appropriate and useful to society, and beautifying our national parks and outdoors.
- We aim to accomplish a 5% flat tax on GDP across the board for every American, Corporation, Charity, or other contributor to the GDP. More on this in the future, but in essence everyone pays 5% with no deductions, No IRS, no income tax filing, no accountants, no loop holes, no exceptions
- We are closing the borders for at least 5 years to all legal and illegal entry. Illegals already in the country will have a 10 year path to citizenship and they will be buying it from the Agency
- There will be a new national card that will house all your money, personal information, and vital ID's. This card will stop theft, crime, and the ability to sneak around the country, cheat on taxes, ensure illegals are registered, will give you the convenience of a single form of ID, put vital information at immediate availability, and is supported by

the most advanced IT and new inventions. It
will save Federal, State, and local authorities
billions of AC and personnel and generate
additional income streams to be passed
along to you.

There is much more to inform you about but as
you can see our plate is plenty full.

You are likely to have some liberties or freedoms
put on hold for a short period during these
transformations.

But, we ask you to heavily weigh the dark path we
were headed down that would have lasted for
generations and the bright future that's upon us.
Many will talk about Big Brother, violation of the
constitution, privacy infringements, and they are
right. There is no other way.

(They have so discretely buried the announcement
of Gun banning, loss of privacy and the freedom
to control your own finances, the crackdown on
illegals, deadbeat Dads and others avoiding
justice. The News media will focus mainly on the
expansion of medical, schools, jobs, and a very
low income tax rate. As they roll out some of the
more shocking or controversial programs they will
claim that everyone was given advance warning.)
Chapter 31 – The Federal Budget, the big expense
slash, and goodbye bureaucrats

As already concluded by the OMB and Treasury
the Agency will have a on going stream of just
over 2.5 trillion VC to operate on annually. They

have another 5 trillion in reserves if needed for new programs, gun buybacks, education, hospitals and medical care. They plan raises to deserving occupations, housing, infrastructure, and job training.

Under President Clinton in 2000 the budget was balanced. The Government spent 2 trillion dollars. Ten years later 2010 Barrack Obama's administration spent 2.16 trillon dollars and we were at war in two countries at least. We were just coming out of the worst recession and recovery in history. Obama even bailed out the economy with a 900 billion stimulus, and the national debt was still down at 14 trillion. As of the takeover September 2024 it more than doubled. In 2024 the Government will spend 3.8 trillion which includes items like the one time Covid recovery Jobs act of 1.9 trillion.
For just a start the army of accountants that have been working for Lucas Malkin and Molaskey for 6 weeks and a team that Alan Blake put together over 2 months ago have come up with the following savings and cutbacks.

Closing Congress (4.1 billion)
Bringing troops home downsizing the military into a "Drone Army" (280 Billion)
That's after spending a new 50 billion on an all Drone Army/Navy/Marines
Defaulting on the National Debt (120 Billion

annual interest savings)
Eliminating 90% of the IRS (10.5 Billion)
Rolling Fema into the Military (6.5 Billion)
Eliminating Census (14.2 Billion every 10 years)
Fraud Savings in Unemployment, Welfare, Snap,
Section 8 etc. (125 Billion)
Reduced Federal Salaries (30.5 Billion)
International Welfare (245 Billion)
Federal Child Tax Credits (15 Billion)
SBA Losses (31 Billion)
Justice Department (5 Billion)
Public Transportation Subsidies (8 Billion)
Post Office (8 Billion)
EPA (6 Billion)
Emergency Rental Assistance (15 Billion)
Federal Unemployment Benefits (45 Billion)
Prescription Drugs (35 Billion)
Corporation Public Broadcasting (2.5 Billion0
Coronavirus Relief (430 Billion)
NIH (3.5 Billion)
Dept of Energy (50 Billion)

This is just a sampling of savings without
detrimentally harming anyone's standard of living
and in some cases programs are replaced by more
cost efficient and effective programs. The VA is
untouched as well as the FAA, Federal Hiways,
Social Security and Medicare.

The immediate savings is 1.67 trillion from the
current inflated budget of 3.8 trillion.

The Agency is very happy with this number. Once released there will be an overwhelming whining and doomsday theories that the Agency is ready to push back on. The biggest voices will be the bureaucrats that have for decades wielded the power of the purse for their egos, special projects, and graft.

The Agency's winning message will be 5% flat tax. An average $15,000 more in the pockets of average income working families, a known business cost of 5% tax added to other costs (investment and new start ups will soar at these rates).
Enhanced medical and educational services for all, no homelessness, no one goes hungry or without shelter, jobs for all, no congressional dysfunction, no wars and lost hero's, plenty of goods on the shelves, a near crime less society, and our adversaries kept in check.

Chapter 32 – The Press struggles to argue

Still after 2 months since the takeover no one can put a handle on whether the Agency is liberal or conservative, white or multi race, religious or atheist. They are conservative and aggressive when it comes to borders, crime, and finances, but quite liberal when it comes to demographics, wealth, social programs, safety nets, the homeless, the unemployed, and many other compassionate causes. The press overall has been very supportive. The divide that they so be lovingly held onto, race, wealth, privilege, sexual preference, etc. has been mostly erased and filled with more anticipation of what is coming next. It's not popular to be pessimistic about the Agency and ratings have showed that right away.

Some of the liberal media still can't give up Trump derangement Syndrome. They spread conspiracy theories that Trumps ghost is alive and well running the Agency. Another CNN anchor insists that Trump spent 4 years dictating and planning his second Presidency and the Agency was implementing it to a tee. Another MSNBC host suggests that Trump survived the gun attack in Sarasota, he never did have an open casket, and that he was the Agency and was running everything from a hiding place.
They point out that Melania and Barron make frequent trips to a highly secretive and secure Chateau in Switzerland that Trump purchased in 2023. Is he hiding there ?

The fact that the Agency triggered the cancellation of the national debt is something that Trump had mentioned on numerous occasions. Trump had been heard saying that in a perfect world to achieve his goals a shutdown of Congress would make things much quicker and seamless. Just coincidence or is he or his legacy the driving force of the Agency.

Chapter 33 – The VC Card. Don't leave home without it

Of all the changes, the VC card will be the most controversial. It will be a love it or hate it proposition. Those that argue against it say it is the biggest government intrusion ever. Most of those people had something to hide. Drug deals, income tax evasion, dead beat Dads, bookies and prostitutes, gun dealers. It breaks all the barriers for civil rights, freedom, and privacy. It is anti American value and totalitarianism at it's best. And they will be vocal up to the point of requiring a trip to the Luciano Las Vegas.

The supporters have a much better argument for the need and benefits. The VC card or something like it was already in the development stages before the takeover. It's a universal card covering just about everything in your life, just short of knowing your thoughts. It goes way past the profiling that Google, Sahara Inc, and Facebook had ever dreamed. The technology is once in a century. The card is about twice the size of a credit card.
The memory card has 8GB of storage. The lithium batteries go up to 1 week without recharging and the batteries charge by solar anytime there is the smallest amount of light. You would have to lock

yourself in a closet to run the batteries down.
 You can also get emergency performance just by laying flat on a small magnet. The cards are linked to a satellite system that covers the globe. There are three backup redundancy clouds that update in real time. Your card reflects a purchase before a clerk can hand you a receipt. They have many windows which the owner and user only access. Most are locked for authorities to use. They are secured by a nine digit number, a retina scan, a fingerprint, and a pin number. They are virtually un-hackable and of no use expect to the owner. Laws are very strict about theft, use by anyone other than the owner, or any form of fraud.

It is mandatory for every person on American soil to have one. There are primary cards for citizens and special cards for illegal residents, and cards for temporary visitors. The VC offices have authority to issue, appoint agents to issue and maintain, and resolve problems or disputes. VC cards must be applied for and issued within 90 days of a new birth.
There are no opt out options and no cherry picking what information goes on your card. Card holders can view their balances, view and print their activity, review their contacts, medical records, medication, criminal history, and it goes on. Only selected VC readers and authorized personnel can access medical records or make edits, The same is true for criminal histories,

licenses, etc.

All vendors, service or retail, medical caregivers, DMV, police, the library, employers, Agency authorized agents, voter registrars, will be furnished readers with retina and fingerprint readers. Card holders can purchase retina and fingerprint readers for their home computers, cars, and cell phones. If you ever misplace your card as long as you have memorized your 10 digit number anyone with a reader and retina & fingerprint recognition can create a transaction without a card.

In short, the cards and accounts are secure and unless someone is holding a gun to your head to supply your retina and fingerprint there is no way for unauthorized transactions. Most card holders will optfor "don't allow charges without retina and fingerprint verification".

The Agency owns the technology, patents, and rights to the systems internationally. They are allowing banks to charge up to a .015% transaction fee and can share any part of that with their customer retailer or service sellers. The Agency charges nothing for the card or the vendor hardware. Internationally they are licensing the technology and anticipate the Agency corporation will take in about 120 billion annually.

The card will carry the following information:

- Your complete identity

- Address
- Phone numbers, ss number
- Picture, fingerprint,, Retina
- Security questions
- Value Rating and Cr Score
- Employer, position/title, previous employers. Military status
- Automobiles registered, insurance information
- Next of Kin, Martial Status, Children, Relatives
- Bank Accts, Savings, Balances, Investments, Retirement accts
- Mortgage Loans, Other Loans, and credit facilities
- Alerts when your over drafting, have upcoming payments due
- Credit facilities like overdraft protection
- Citizen Status; birth place
- Final wishes & directives
- Medical Records, blood type, Immunizations, Doctors, Surgeries, Allergies
- Legal passport

Without a VC card your in a no mans land. You can't drive, by gas or anything else. You can't rent or purchase, can't work or make money, can't take public transportation, can't have a phone or internet access and you can't receive medical treatment

If you are a deadbeat Dad, your now paying up automatically

If you have a warrant for your arrest they will be finding you soon

If your license or registration are due you are politely reminded

If you have a pending appt with your doctor you are reminded

If you have a Income Tax payment due you are given prior notice then it is deducted

If you move you only make one call or notification and all contacts are alerted

If you are trying to improve your personal Value Rating the system helps you accomplish this

You can locate your VC card by GPS or you can locate your family members by GPS

You don't receive statements in the mail if you don't want them

Your income taxes are filed automatically , you are allowed to review them and you are alerted in advance if you are going to be a little short or have a refund

The Feds, State and local authorities are saving billions in manpower, printing and mailing, nothing slips through the cracks, everybody pays their fair share. Bad guys are apprehended real quickly. Before long many western civilizations are using the technology and while they may have a new name for it, our their currency the benefits are the same. The VC is the most accepted and often required form of payment worldwide.

Chapter 34 – The Big Bust

Its March of 2025 about a month before the Presidential election. The previous electorate are whining about their power. The freedom party as it is called is having rallies about their rights and Big Brother, The Agency. Crime is almost negligible. Over 300 million VC cards have been issued and the last naysayers will have no choice in about 2 weeks to get signed up or they quit basically living. Quarterly interest payments on the National Debt, 35 Trillion are due in a couple of weeks. With the banks ready to transform the currency from Dollars to VC credits the Agency releases it's next shocking press announcement.

Citizens, Non Citizens, Foreign Nationals, and Oversea Adversaries & Friends.
You have trusted the American Dollar and the security of investing in America for centuries and we thank you for that.

We take no pleasure to announce today that the American Government is Bankrupt. We have given of our monetary strength to all nations for decades. We have arrived at every national disaster, defended our allies and never asked for anything in return.
Our generosity and compassion has resulted in our financial ruin. As of Monday morning the US Dollar will be obsolete. panicking or trading irrationally will do no good.

The US Dollar will be replaced by Value Credits.
All American citizens will be allowed to redeem
dollars, both currency, passbook savings, bank
credits at the following rate.

0–$10,000   1 VC per US Dollar
$10,001 to $100,000 `````.80 VC to US Dollar
$100,001 to 1 million   .50 VC to US Dollar
1 million or more   .33 VC to US Dollar
This is for American citizens only. Otherwise your
US currency is worth nothing and your banking
account balances cannot be transferred to VC
either.

Stocks and bonds will reset at 1 VC to 1 Dollar

If you hold US Notes or Treasury Bonds
Americans and American traded and owned
investments will be given Agency stock according
to the above formula with the exception being 1
million or more in Treasury notes will receive .50
of VC stock. VC stock will be traded on the
NASDAQ under the appreciation of VCS.

If you are American and have not secured your VC
card yet you better do it soon. Re tailors will
continue to take US currency for 30 days. Banks
are open extra hours to redeem your hard
currency onto your VC card. All exchange of US
currency will cease on March 31st and the

remaining cash will have 48 hours to be redeemed by your bank into VC. Any trade after that date of US currency is forbidden by law.

No interest will be paid on US foreign debt from this day forward and all foreign debt in US dollars or any promissory note is canceled.

We realize that many of you will see immediate depreciation of your wealth, your retirement accounts and portfolios. This is much better than the imminent default that would have created a 0 zero value for your investments moving forward. At least you should have some of your investments in order, VC to buy supplies and necessities, a good job, an income going forward, and a clear prospect with American hard work and ingenuity we will be back stronger than ever.

Thank You

The Agency

Chapter 35 – Fallout around the world

Within days of the September 14, 2024 takeover the Agency ordered the XL pipeline be restarted. They also restarted the border wall. All previous oil leases were renewed and Anwar drilling was back on track. By December the US was supplying all the oil and natural gas it could use domestically. They had regained their position by the end of February as a key supplier of gas and natural gas around the world. The price of a barrel of oil dropped back from $115 to $48. Refiners and drillers were making a modest profit, Unleaded gasoline was back to $2.35 a gallon and much of the world relied on the U.S. for this stability.

Countries had to take into account their need for oil and also military contract purchases that their was no other source for, like drones, fighter jets, and submarines. They needed to show their disappointment and disgust for the debt cancellation. Demonstrate what it had done to their economies but not totally irritate the Agency and turn them against them. Many countries recalled their ambassadors and kicked out US ambassadors. According to one Agency spokesman, that was OK, because we were looking for an excuse to recall our missions anyway. Just a small list of losers China 1.1 trillion, Japan 1.2 trillion, Taiwan 234 billion, Belgium 234 billion, Brazil, 255 billion, Switzerland 261 billion, UK 431 billion, and it goes on.

World markets and currencies plunged over 20% on the news, a net wealth loss of over 30 Trillion. The Chinese Yuan rose 10% on the news as several investors saw it as a safe haven for now. The damage would have been worse if the U.S. wasn't sitting on such massive oil reserves and 6 trillion in Gold Reserve.

The new national debt which was traded for Agency stock was 6 Trillion a mere 1/5th of the previous day, Without this drastic move all the nations and foreign corporate investors would have lost it all anyway but the American consumer and investor may have never come back. It was the correct thing to do under the circumstances. By the summer of 2025 with all the changes and many bright moves by the US Treasury and sticking to the plans of the Agency, the US economy was humming, exports were up, the VC had hit 1.20 against the Canadian dollar and .95 VC against the Euro which was right back where the US dollar was just 4 months earlier. The dow Jones which had hit a high of 42,000 in December of 2024 then pulled back to 32,000 right after the default was now back to 38,000 and predicted to go much higher.

Chapter 36 – Housing Demand and Inflation

With energy dropping so repetitiously and other food and leisure costs stabilizing the overall inflation rate was at 1.5% annually, a manageable number. The one stand out cost that failed to budge was building supplies, especially raw lumber. Earl Molasky with Mr. Blake created a plan to bring this under control. Their was a big demand for new housing and resales with wages way up, zero unemployment, and low interest rates. The U.S. entered a contract with Russia for

50 million tons of timber, coming mostly from Siberia in the form of fir and pine; both good for house building. Container after container arrived at west coast ports where existing mills worked around the clock and the Agency entered the business with U.S. Timber Corp opening two new mega mills. By July of 2025 a 2x4 by eight foot, common grade which had reached 8.50 VC now dropped to 2.25 VC and a sheet of plywood that was selling for 60 VC you could now buy at Home Depot for 6.99 VC.

Existing homes sales had reached a medium of over 400,000 VC with very few in select parts of the country under 300,000 VC. People were not moving as much. During the 2018 to 2024 period a combination of Wok policies and high taxes in liberal states saw a mass exodus to places like Florida, Tennessee, and Texas.

If people could afford to move they already had. The Agency enacted a new closing protocol for residential real estate that reduced the expense and time by less than ½. Realtors were no longer allowed to charge more than 2% combined in commissions and they still made out well with the higher selling prices. Adding to the cost was the sellers 5% flat tax to the Feds; no cost basis deductions and no exceptions. New home builders were taking orders 24 months out as a whole generation became employed and qualified for loans. A new generation of wealth building was taking place. With the new flat tax almost every working American, which was 98% of the non retired population was saving on average 15,000 VC per household. The flat tax generated 114 billion in tax revenue on 7.1 million sales in one year. This was a windfall as well for the Treasury which was staying within their current budgets. Not far off was the HAC plan (Housing for America Corp) where the Agency would become a planned community developer

Chapter 37 –The new federal Surplus and the Lefts long awaited wish list

Dating back to 2019 and the emergence of the Progressive left's agenda they had been trying to pass many entitlement programs through congress that all failed. The one the Agency liked the most was the Child Day Care that would allow millions of new Moms and moms that left the workforce during Covid to come back in the workforce. The Agency is going to use 60 billion of the new 5% revenue from home sales to offer grants for businesses to build on–site day care and ACE (After School Education) facilities. This means that an assembly line worker, an administrator, or a Sales Rep can let their children off in the morning and pick them up when their shift is done, at the same location as work. Any older children can be dropped by their school buses at the centers so the family is all united just before dinner time. These centers need to be staffed by the companies receiving the grants. The Agency can float construction bonds for about four times the amount of their cash contribution. This would mean about 3.5 million grants of an average of 200,000 VC each. The businesses get the benefit of adding the RE value to their balance sheet after 3 years of operation. This will bring an approximate 5.5 million workers off the sidelines and dearly needed to supply the demand in the country. The Children get pre K education and special tutoring after school plus physical education and sports. These funds are targeted first at low income and underprivileged neighborhoods and companies. As part of the Agencies program to get as many Americans into home ownership it's clearly an advantage to have a rwo income family for qualifying for a mortgage. As many Dads evolved as Stay at home Dads dating back to the Covid epidemic this program is open to fathers as well. Additionally the centers will employee about 4 million childcare specialists which will be trained by the Agency job training program and for the Mom's that previously claimed she couldn't work because of parenting duties or physical limitations just about anyone can handle the rigors of holding a baby or watching kids on a playground. The kids would get extra mentoring, very much needed physical exercise, learn new technologies, keep them out of trouble and away from any bad influences and make lifelong friends. This program offers so many opportunities as dictated by the new "Workfare" law which simply is no work, no entitlements.

The other 60 billion VC in new taxable sales on real estate will go to the Corporation for American Health & Wellness with another 40 billion VC in investment from the Agency board.

Chapter 38 – Corporation for American Health & Wellness

The Agency motto from day one has been, "If its not broken, don't fix it." The VA operates at about 80% efficiency and as long as veterans are getting quality care that's all the Agency cares about. Obama care is a messed up plan, the insurance companies are the biggest winners of this overly bureaucratic program, but again the Agency has bigger fish to fry. The best answer to national health care are the employer paid or subsidized plans which are keenly negotiated, part of an employees compensation, and cost the taxpayers nothing. Still there is a need for of service and prevention for the lowest 15% income workers. Additionally illegal immigrants and non citizens which hit 35 million under the Biden administration show up a hospital emergency room for every mosquito bite and are giving treatment. This has clogged the whole purpose of

emergency and trauma centers purpose and ultimately cost about 500% more. There is literally no way to turn away this group and refuse medical attention so it's better to deal with it in the most economical way.
With the rewriting of the federal budget, the tremendous savings of over 1.8 trillion VC in federal expenditures, many windfall new collections, and promises made by the Agency, the medical landscape is changing rapidly.

Dr. Len Parsons with all of his government, business, and medical experience, plus great common sense, is at the helm of the Corporation for American Health. It is owned by the Agency, the largest private company of the Agency, and traded on the NASDAQ.
A big focus of the Agency getting 100% support is to end homelessness forever. Homelessness is really more of a sickness than anything. Also the mentally ill walking our streets is the number one contributor to violent crime, drug abuse, alcoholism, and family abuse.
The CAH is buying up abandoned medical facilities, hospitals, and residential group opportunities. It is building facilities in lower income and under served neighborhoods.
They have reinvented the sanatorium model for mental illness. Homeless people are rounded up and taken for physical and mental evaluations. They receive the best medical treatment and cures.

They are housed and mentored by other recovering and recovered addicts, psychiatrists, and therapists. They are given new clothing and hobbies. They are receiving job training and upon graduation are given job placements and housing with repeated and regular monitoring. Another benefit of the VC card. This groups behavior and purchasing can be monitored in real time.

The programs are 90% successful at keeping people that would have preferred suicide previously; employed, enjoying family life, showing immense self pride and confidence and mentoring other misguided citizens out from darkness of depression. Spirituality plays a big role. Many recovered patients have found a calling in preaching the Bible and community service. Some are holding down 150,000 VC annual careers. The illegal drug Milesets have dried up for the cartels and petty drug pushers, the few that were left. There are some that had wandered too far from reality and they are permanently and compassionately housed for their protection. Big cities once strewn with hypodermics, homeless in tents and door ways, feces, petty theft, and the constant harassment of passer-bys now have their charm and desirability back. In addition, the CAH has walk-in clinics in depressed neighborhoods, and rural areas, excellent regional hospitals and out patient services, family planning and adoption programs. The Corporation has enlisted on average 100,000 new medical trainees per year into their medical schools and career training facilities with new medical school students getting concurrent residency with their studying programs. The facility research centers have joined the most prestigious laboratories and pharmaceutical companies in developing cutting edge treatments and drugs.

Within 1 year between the Medicaid savings and the fraud that it was famous for, the 60 billion annually contributed from home sales, licensing for new medicines, and the sales of new medical equipment, the CAH is turning a profit. It's stock has almost doubled and is a sweetheart with the retirement funds and conservative portfolios. How do you solve more problems with one plan: Homelessness, Mental Health, Under Insured and Uninsured, Develop new life saving therapy's and equipment, train 10,000 of thousands of medical students, employ over 400,000 without disrupting current markets, and do it at a profit.

Chapter 39 – The American outdoors

By 2026 work participation is above 95%. If you take away the parents that choose to have a stay at home parent that number is closer to 98%. Americans are working and working hard. Inventing, building, innovating, buying homes and adult toys, and doing it without OPEC or cheap Chinese imitations. The Agency encourages all private industry companies to offer their employees paid vacations. The Agency is always careful not to exceed industry standards in their pay in a commitment to not compete with American Industry. Their goals have always been to fill the gaps where the private sector cannot keep up with demand, has no interest to enter the field, or fill holes created due to limiting imports. The Agency Corporations use their generous vacation packages often as a lure to recruit good workers. Due to numerous more Covid variants emerging in the world, a world still very much pissed off by our debt default, and a continuing threat by terrorists, travel into the U.S. is almost non existent. Travel to foreign countries is on an emergency basis only with permission. That leaves the mainland US, the US Virgin Islands, Hawaii and Alaska as travel alternatives for vacations. Disneyworld, Univerisal and other amusement parks are by reservation only. Hawaii had a rebirth following the pandemic and is booked solid all year long. Many of the Agency's board are avid outdoors men and woman. They have dedicated human and financial resources to the National Park system for renovations, expansions, and are adding parks, all with a tentative eye to the pristine nature and fragility of wild areas. Parks are geting expanded camp sites and cabins, supply resources (food etc.), hiking trails, water access, ranger involvement and orientation and updated reservation systems. People are taking to the American outdoors.

Accept for July and August availability is good whether its by a lake, the ocean, in the woods, or famous destinations like Yosemite and Yellowstone. Cabellas and all it's competitors have doubled in size and American manufacturers of outdoor apparel and hardware are hot items on the exchanges.

Chapter 40 – Worse than 9/11

We knew that during the Biden years of open borders 2020-2024 that many jihadists, terrorists, and sympathizers of the Koran had entered the country illegally. Almost all scattered, changed their country of origin and took up normal carreers and families to assimilate. Some 25 Al Qaeda terrorists made it in through the southern border in 2021 with the specific goal of launching an attack on the U.S. They were well funded by Al Qaeda and the Taliban. They resided in different parts of the U.S. and never communicated by phone or computer. Communication was done by the postal service and then in code. They purchased a small toy manufacturer in Detroit where they developed and sold children's bowling sets. The bowling balls, about 4 inches in diameter, were modified to hold a powder bladder, a small explosive, and a remote detonator. They manufactured anthrax in two other locations and would transfer the anthrax only by personal vehicle. They picked July 3, 2023 for their attack.

July 4th although symbolic was no good because people were off work. They selected all together 80 sites to detonate their anthrax.

NYC subway, Wall Street, two baseball parks, The Smithsonian, a large auto plant with one main entrance & exit. Disneyworld, Universal, the Lincoln memorial, two cruise ships, Bourbon Street, Mall of the Americas, Hartsfield Atlanta Airport, Logan Airport, Penn Station, and the New Hampshire State Fair were all on the list. They are coordinated for 5 pm EST attack. An estimated 2000 people were within the shock range of the mini bombs. Because of the nature of the bio chemical particles they can travel another 300 feet and enter an air conditioning systems affecting thousands. Also people that have walked through the Anthrax then spread it wherever they go all the way into their homes.

A national alert is sounded, cell phones ring with emergency messages, The amber alert system is mobilized. People are advised to shelter in place. Hospitals are put on alert. The news is carrying information on the cities and places the bombs were exploded. The office of emergency management releases the following information.

"At 5 pm eastern time today simultaneous explosions containing anthrax were released at key transportation and entertainment locations throughout the U.S. Although anthrax can be lethal in small doses it causes respiratory illnesses that are treatable. Hazmat units have been dispatched to all effected areas and are in the process of a cleanup. If you were in or near (300 feet) of any of the locations listed in this alert from 4 pm EST to 6 pm EST please follow these instructions. Do not travel, shelter in place. Do not go to emergency unless you are having trouble breathing. Remove the cloths and shoes you were wearing and place them in a sealed plastic garbage bag. Shower thoroughly. Place your towel in a plastic garbage bag as well. Miles the bags with an (X) and place away from humans or animals. If you were in close contact with other members of your household have them repeat the same steps above. Call the following number. 800-655-5555 and report your personal information, where you were, at what time, and your mode of travel from the scene. Report any symptoms you may be having. First responders are equipped with hand held assays to detect the presence of B. anthracis (anthrax) spores. If this field test is positive you would be directed to a health facility for more detailed laboratory testing. There is no reason to panic, please just follow the instructions of your emergency management team and law enforcement. " Regional hospitals in Atlanta, NYC, Washington DC, Boston and Orlando are packed with people panicked not following instructions. The police have blocked emergency entrances and are shoving people away from the hospitals. The news shows people screaming for help, most with no symptoms at all.

The worst exposure was in the theme parks where thousands of families walked through the powder before security discovered it all and closed the parks. Every car, cab, bus, train, hotel, restaurant that could have come into contact needs to be shut down and inspected with field assays. The Agency has declared a state of emergency.

Within two days some order is restored. Most of the bombed areas have been cleared of any harmful bacteria. Drive up sites are established to test cars, people, pets, and items that may have come into contact. Special removal vehicles are dispatched to pick up bags with (X's) typically in driveways or by appointment. The theme parks and baseball stadiums and museums will be closed for two months for further cleaning and inspection. Wall street was closed for one week. Bourbon street and the Mall of the Americas might as well have been closed as not one customer can be found. It's truly 3 months before everything is back to normal and the incidents are getting in the rear view mirror in peoples minds.

Over 1800 civilians are killed, 6,000 injured, many with permanent disabilities and some loss of mental capacity. The cost to businesses, wall street, and law enforcement is in the billions. The Agency doesn't care about being Wok and makes a point that it was extremest Muslims again from a foreign country. The FBI and other intelligence agencies are ordered to double down on any middle eastern immigrants, legal or not, and approves spying on mosques.

Nobody is arguing or questioning anymore the Agency's decision to close our borders and not allow foreign travel in the United States.

Chapter 41 – Immigration and the border

From the day of the takeover by the Agency, September 14, 2024, National Guard troops from both the federal Corps and States were sent to the border. Army, Marine, Coast Guard, and even Navy troops were deployed and their equipment and support systems followed within days. Now most of the military might is stationed along the border. Generals Sanderson and Bokanison developed a plan which was submitted to the Agency for approval. It included immediate completion of the wall. Any foreign nationals traveling daily or with some frequency at busy ports like Yuma, Brownsville, and El Paso were ordered to stay in Mexico and failure to return to Mexico will be subject to getting stranded in the U.S. for an unknown period. New cars, Avocados, Oreo Cookies, and appliances will be getting stalled and most will not be allowed entry. The usual stream of trucks coming in from Mexico is reduced to a trickle. Military bases that do not have a strategic geographical purpose in their current locations are relocated to the southern border. Drone and other surveillance is deployed to the Canadian border. The U.S. is locked down from the rest of the world. All international flights are canceled and green card holders and tourists are given 72 hours to leave the country.

Any shipping containers that are allowed to be unloaded in U.S. ports are unloaded at the dock and thoroughly inspected. Large amounts of drugs, guns, and other contraband are discovered which only increases the Customs inspections and authority to refuse cargo from overseas.

For almost four years Joe Biden has allowed 5 million immigrants to enter the U.S. not vetted. The 2023 Anthrax bombers came in this way. For those that would argue that we are a nation of immigrants, well, Biden filled the quota for about ten years moving forward. The push is really on to increase the U.S. manufacturing base to replace all the imports that are now not allowed to enter.

All residents of the U.S. including illegals are required to get a VC card. Failure to do so will result in immediate deportation for non citizens. Finally the government has a true handle on the depth, location, incomes, and all pertinent information for aliens. Aliens are forced to enter programs to become citizens over a ten year period. They will pay $100 per person, per month,

to the Agency, in addition to the 5% flat tax and any other fees, without exception. If they cannot support themselves or pay the citizenship fees on time when due then they are deported.
Any illegal felons are either deported or jailed depending on the severity of their crime.

Foreign travel for Americans is not safe and too difficult to monitor. The U.S. has almost no overseas missions or embassy's anymore. Several variants of Covid are still being passed around in third world countries and some Western European Countries. The Agency has committed to reopening traffic on a country by country basis once the threat of terrorists and disease are diminished but ordinary immigration will not return for some time.

Chapter 42 – The American Dream of Home Ownership

Home ownership was 67.4% in 2020. It had grown to 69% until the Biden administrations poor policies saw interest rates go over 6% for thirty year mortgages. Lumber and building materials more than doubled and wages shrunk with inflation requiring larger down payments and stricter underwriting guidelines. In 2025 with the resetting of the currency, expansion of the U.S. timber trade and forestation. Plus imports from Russia, and new supply chain availability of everything from shingles, to screwdrivers, to dryers. Demand was taking off for a whole generation of renters that wanted to be homeowners. The traditional builders, Dell Webb, Lennar, Citation, etc. could only fill a small part of this demand. The Agency had fast tracked their trade school education and were turning out 10's of thousands of skilled journeymen and journey women in carpentry, sheet metal, electrical, plumbing, electrical, roofing and all building trades. The traditional builders were shy about building higher density projects, especially since they could sell all the single family homes they could build. The Agency formed Housing for America Corp., a construction company targeted at building planned communities.

Still reeling from the riots of 2019 that went on sporadically until 2024, low income and minority neighborhoods had very few home ownership opportunities. In 1995 Tom & Ann Cousins, philanthropists, envisioned the new East Lake community. It was an impoverished, minority, and high crime suburb of Atlanta. Twenty six years later it is a model for planned communities offering attractive housing, parks, community centers, charter schools, lakes, walking paths, clubs, and a clear vision of pride of ownership. The schools have the highest graduation rates and GP's.

Alan Blake and the board of the Agency used the

East Lake model when developing their new construction company Housing for America (HAC) and plans for contained communities.

They purchased whole city blocks and forced by eminent domain any unwilling sellers. Projects (a bad word associated with minority slums), Developments ranged from 10 acres up to 400 acres with multi-unit town homes, mostly single level. They had 50 developments in the building stage with 25,000 residences to be completed by the end of 2027. The developments had parks, walking paths, mature landscaping, lakes, baseball and soccer fields, tennis courts, volleyball pits, picnic and BBQ areas, swimming pools, underground parking, lighting, 24 hour security and cameras. Each unit had a panic button to a guard shack which was every 200 yards. The Charter Schools, pre K to 12th grade were the best in the country. The athletic programs were turning out superstars in all sports. They had shopping areas, restaurants, hair cutting salons, and a Corp for American Health clinic for regular doctor and emergency 24 hr service. Many had community centers and Centers for the performing Arts where they encouraged drama, music, and art programs. The communities had clubs and groups for the promotion and entertainment of almost everything. The community celebrated together for Christmas, Halloween, 4th of July, and Labor Day. They were only available for sale, no renters. Owners needing to get out were purchased back from the Agency and resold. Each owner was required to do 20 hours a month of improvements, repairs, landscaping, field maintenance, etc. A two bedroom town home started at 190,000 VC. Medium family incomes had progressed to 80,000 VC and most working couples reported 120,000 VC or more. With interest back in the 3.25% range a 190,000 mortgage was about 830 VC a month plus taxes and Insurance. This was a little less than average rentals. There was a waiting list to purchase.

Most single parents or couples had no problem qualifying and with down payment assistance getting in cost as little at 3000 VC. The Agency was buying property and planning communities as quick as the labor force would support the developments. Graduates from the Agency's living skills training programs were required to work for the HAC corporation for three years as a payback for their free internship and training. They were paid market wages and most stayed on after the three years and advanced in the Agency. The Agency had a 10% return on investment after they paid their required 5% flat tax from the sales. This perpetual circle of funding, pay a little now for future development was a great corporate model. From the 25,000 units closing in 2027 they would contribute 25 billion in tax revenue back to the general fund which then would fund more planned communities and more development for

Corporation for American Health facilities.
Call it socialism, some called it Marxist policy, others communism, but whatever you wanted to call it, it works. People are working, raising families, gaining wealth, contributing in their communities, and practicing their chosen faith. For once in a long while the news is full of good stories and not so many bad stories.

Chapter 43- The Luciano is closing shop for bad guys

The High Dessert State Prison, north of Las Vegas, was purchased by the Agency in 2025. It's location is perfect for high risk to minimum security inmates. It's capacity was 4,175 inmates. The Agency began immediate expansions to take the facilities capacity up to 15,000 inmates. With a couple new sections finished it's time to give Mr Luciano his hotel back. With limited choices for vacationers due to the shutdown of overseas travel, Las Vegas like Hawaii and other popular destinations is humming. Luciano deserves a chance to cash in on this. He has about 300 remaining low and medium security detainees and these will either be released or transferred to the High Dessert Facility. It will take about 30 million VC to put his hotel back in order. Local police, sheriffs, and states are told to keep their DUI's, domestic violent prisoners, any child under the age of 15, and minor drug possession offenders.

The Agency wants your worst. The gang bangers, fire arm violators, robbers other than petty theft, car jackers, assault cases and certainly murder and rape cases. A new term was popularized in the 2020 election. It was "court packing". It's what the liberals planned to do to get their power back. Trump had appointed more federal judges and Supreme Court judges than any other President. Still, there were prosecutors and judges letting hardened criminals out with no bail just to re-offend, often including murder. Among the other powers taken up by the Agency, only the Agency would be appointing judges and prosecutors until further notice. Stiffer sentences, no bails, speedy trials, and good public awareness all worked to keep criminals from repeat offending. Most crimes the Agency had no tolerance for were referred for Federal prosecution. The states liked the Fed for taking the financial responsibility. This in itself was another driving force to crime reduction. Overall crime had been reduced by 70%. No one will remember what a gun looked like in another 24 months. The Agency rehabilitation had a different look than any other ever tried before. They start with the premise that all people, all souls, are redeemable, can be made good again and that sticks and carrots are the best tools. Firstly, there are three levels of prisons. Maximum security houses the most violent and uncooperative prisoners. Not that they are not able to be rehabilitated but it's more work and less serious offenders should not be subject to jail violence. Medium security is kind of a purgatory for serious non-violent offenders that need to prove that they are willing to change. They need to earn their way into minimum security and possible early release.

Minimum security is for offenders that are trying to prove that they will not re-offend once on the outside, they show some remorse for their mistakes, they present no hostility, and will cooperate and join in any program the system has in store for them. The one thing that is common in all levels of offenders is usually a lack of parental guidance, often a single parent, sometimes alcoholism involved, and a good chance of family and spousal abuse. Another words broken homes. The other thing that is prevalent is the lack of a good education. Young adults often turn to the street when they have a lack of engagement with education, the system lets them skate by until they either graduate with very low basic abilities or they drop out of school. They had no mentors or discipline.

The Agency has a turn the clock back approach. The whole plan is individualize for each prisoner and goals are set. The system is candid, each prospect knows whats expected of them.

The intake quantifies the prisoners education level, family history, and any family peers that can be involved. They start education at whatever level they got previously left behind. It could be 2nd

grade or freshman in high school. They are given a fast track goal to achieve high school level competency. They concurrently are introduced to about 20-30 career paths.

This is about the same program path the CAH, Corporation for American Health, has rolled out for the homeless. Within 2 months for minimum security and no more than 4 months for maximum security prisoners they are concurrently taking the basic 3 r's and also training in construction fields, medicine tech positions, business or sales, administration, computer science, auto mechanics, law enforcement, forest and agricultural management, psychology and therapy for addiction and lifestyle change. The teachers and staff are very clear about the positions to aspire for, including the base and potential salaries. If the enrollee's complete all training and courses and can convince the parole board of their new dedication to a clean and non criminal life, they are guaranteed a job by the Agency, plus housing, medical, and continued therapy and support. They are not allowed to locate in their old hood. The goal is for them to create new associations and friendships and not fall back into the cesspool that got them to their worst moment in life. Some inmates have gone on to pass the Bar and become lawyers. Some entered medical school on Agency scholarships after paying their dues to society. Some moved on to become ministers and even Rabbi's or Priests.

The healing and inspiring programs of the prisons have a strong focus on faith and redemption, regardless of any previous denomination.
Staying clean and obeying the laws works hand in hand with the gospels. The Agency's recidivism rate is less than 4%. Many graduates of the Agency rehabilitation system have gone on to become famous. Most were young enough when intervention took place that
they got married and probably had children. They all dedicate time in the community working with youth to keep them out of gangs and drugs.
Of all the successes of the Agency this is the one along with the Agency planned communities that the board and Alan Blake are most proud of. Anyone can make a stock quadruple or create millions of AC's but saving life's is the ultimate in personal accomplishment. Mr Blake live streams the graduations and the release of both prisoners and homeless graduates as these are his favorite topics of discussion.

Chapter 44 – Decoupling with China

Already by 2022 the capacity of the ports to handle Asian imports had exceeded any reasonable turn around time for deliveries of goods and parts. It was now taking 120 days from departure to arrival in U.S. warehouses for goods from China. The US economy had been stalled by idle manufacturing plants waiting for chips and other parts supplies to finish everything from cars, to electronics, to home whiskey stills. Knowing that serious tariff's were also just down the road when the Republicans took Congress back over in 2023, American manufacturers and marketing companies were wising up and sourcing more of their parts and supply chains from US companies. In 2020 the Chinese averaged over 1 million containers a month delivered into the US economy. By the end of 2023 this was down to ½ million containers a month. US importers were warned that sometime in the future they would need to out source to different producing nations or even better bring home their production. Shortly after the takeover in September of 2024 the Agency appointed William Fence as the "Make it in America" czar and he formed a team to work directly with importers and US manufacturers to bring production back to the US.

With the down sizing of the US Military, downsizing Federal payrolls, and the aggressive turnout of trained, ready to employee high school and college kids, plus with 100 of thousands of Moms returning to the workplace, the US had an ample labor force to fill the new production, administrative, and management needs that were being created. Again, a big win for the US treasury with 5% of all the goods being produced going to the general fund and 5% of all personal income.

William Fence and his team found many

alternatives for large and entrepreneurial companies seeking to replace Chinese supply lines. Often at 30% higher costs that would be passed on to consumers. The US consumer had come to accept that toys, cloths, household items and electronics were all going to cost more and they appreciated the value of goods and got longer life from everything they purchased. By 2027 Chinese exports were down to 100,000 containers a month, one tenth of what was being imported just 5 years earlier. All the medical supply lines of prescription, OTC, and medical hardware had been moved to US production. This was the biggest concern for the Agency. The resisting crowd of producers and marketers of Chinese goods would be a small blip on the radar if we ever 100% decoupled. And, they would mostly scramble and survive the embargo.

China had refused to pullback out of Taiwan. They now controlled all of Hong Kong due to Biden's weakness in foreign policy. They were beating us in space and we never want to share a missile exchange with them. They continue to enslave Western China Muslims despite all the UN resolutions. And we longer allow travel there as they have kidnapped our tourists and business people. All the embassies in the US have been closed.

The Chinese people have attempted many takeovers of the communist party and been put down several times in bloodbaths that killed tens of thousands of martyrs. The Yuan is worth nothing in foreign markets. The rich Chinese have fled to Europe or South America often paying 5 to 10 million VC for citizen ship. The U.S. Value Credit is the number one currency in the world especially if your buying crude or natural gas . Famine is occurring all over China and the CCP is barely holding on. The U.S. is concerned that if pushed into a corner the CCP may start a war in the pacific.

It's time to serve the divorce papers and cut off all trade with China. The U.S. treasury has enough funds to subsidize the American farmers through a trade transition and will assist at finding other Milesets for the export of soy, corn, and sugar while keeping our farmers afloat.

Chapter 45 – The New Military

There were 1.4 million active Military personnel when the Agency took over. Bringing troops back from Korea, Germany, and shrinking other overseas bases like Guam, Italy, Spain, the UK, and too many to mention, troop reduction gradually went down to 800,000, About half of these were deployed to the new bases on the border. Not a drop of drugs, weapons, or human trafficking had taken place in the last 9 months, as of 2026. The Mexican cartels and the Cocaine business from South America totally dried up. Unfortunately it took drastic measures like locking up our borders and immigration, tourism suffered a little, and many consumer goods got more expensive. The Agency was able to train and position all returning troops into excellent paying careers. They returned at the height of low mortgages. With all the other Veteran perks there was nothing to complain about. Many transitioned into the Border Patrol, local law enforcement, the DEA and FBI.

It was always very hard watching Al Sha Bob kidnap 100 school children or third world dictators kill their own people, but the Agency had made a pledge to stay out of other peoples and countries wars and internal strife. The last justifiable war was WWII, possibly our mission in Kuwait which was successful and quick.

There was way too many conflicts the last three decades with a tremendous loss of American life, blood, and treasury. Quite possibly it was the middle east wars expense that tipped the scales on the need to file a U.S. bankruptcy. It was time for the other western civilizations to step up and defend the defenseless. The military budget was cut from 736 billion to 290 billion. This made it possible to fund the numerous changes to American life. A balanced budget and strong economy, medical for all, jobs & housing, homelessness abated, food and energy independence, and much more. There were still plenty of outside threats. To protect the Americans the military went 90% techno. Raytheon,

Lockheed, Boeing, and others were set free to develop the most sophisticated drones the world had ever seen. The next war would be conducted from a monitor with play station controllers. Thousands of sharp, driven, and well coordinated gamers were enlisted and furthered their skills under the guidance of Space Command. Military recruiters travel all the international DOTA 2 conventions and competitions offering lucrative jobs in Space Command. Another Trump dream that was very insightful. The U.S. had a fleet of over 2500 drones. Everything from the size of a breadbox up to drone jets that carried multiple MOAB's.

The defense department had strategically maintained relationships in Japan, Australia, bases in Guam & Alaska, the Balkans, and the Indian Ocean. At a moments notice either the fleet of constant network flyovers by drones, about 300 of the fleet, or quickly deployed drones from multiple bases, we could confront almost any attack in the world. Often described as the Bubble Gum Corps, these 20 somethings were really good at what they did. They survaild the world with the network of satellites, reported to commanders, flew armed drones to hot spots, and always hit their targets.

In the summer of 2024 the Chinese made a move on Taiwan and Biden did nothing but watch. Not even a threat of retaliation. China knew it had a

Carte Blanche to the South Pacific. When Don Jr. won the Presidency in April of 2025 he warned his Chinese counterparts not to proceed with any further aggression.

Australia in the meanwhile had to kick several Chinese fishing fleets out of it's territorial offshore limits for poaching and destroying the fishery supply. The Chinese were belligerent and didn't heed the warnings. After a heated afternoon of cat and mouse just off the shores of Cairns the Aussie Navy shot and sunk a fishing boat with a crew of 12.

In retaliation China set up a naval blockade outside Brisbane blocking all container and passenger traffic with a fleet of about 30 destroyers, submarines, and two aircraft carriers. Australia invokes the ANZUS, a military defense treaty between the US, New Zealand, and Australia that promises an attack on one is like an attack on all three. New Zealand responds with what little Navy it has. Don Jr. sends warnings to China to cease the blockade or we will get involved. Nothing changes over a week period as pressure mounts for the U.S. to help out. After weighing all the possible outcomes Don Jr. decides to free up the blockade by damaging two Chinese air craft carriers.

He orders two B52 bombers to drop MOAB's (Mother of all Bombs) on the carriers decks. The hits are so explosive the bombs penetrate all 6 decks and leave a hole the size of a semi truck in the bottom of their hulls. The ships sink within 20 minutes and very few of the crew are picked up in the shark infested waters over the following hours.

Score: US casualties : 0   Chinese casualties : Est 6,000

The next day US intelligence satellites pickup 4 missile sites in western China that have raised their battery of supersonic missiles to a ready position. The US has gone to Defcon 5 and peeled back the silo covers on 800 ballistic nuclear missiles. After 10 tense hours of situation room planning and speculation Don Jr sends a message to the Chinese premier, "Lower your missiles into a flat position taking them off line and we will close out silo covers and go to Defcon 3". Minutes later the satellites show the Chinese missiles being retracted into a flat standby position and the US keeps their part of the bargain.

It's been 7 years since that near Armageddon encounter in the summer of 2025 and not one conflict with the Chinese has come up. Don Jr. called their bluff in a high stakes game and they folded.

Orders for US drones with the US aviation industry hit all time highs in 2027. Between five major producers and an army of smaller tech support companies, overseas contracts were totaling 350 billion in deliveries a year. A small concession of being the worlds defense supplier, the Agency and Treasury were getting 5% income tax on these sales, another 17.5 billion VC for upgrading the Corporation for American Health and the HAC Housing for America Corp.

Chapter 46 – The second gun buyback

In March of 2025 the Agency held a gun buyback day. They offered $700 for revolvers, $800 for rifles & shotguns, and $1,000 for long guns. The VC currency was still 4 weeks away. They collected 50 million guns at a cost of 40 billion dollars. They announced a new buyback for April of 2027. They were increasing the price by 200 VC. At 900 VC to 1,200 VC per firearm this is about 40% more than the new price. It made it ever more tempting to people that no longer feared for their security. With crime down by 80% it didn't seem as necessary to have a gun. Family of some of the bad guys know where there is 3, maybe 5 guns stored from the old days. This is 4,000 VC quick cash, no questions asked, just for the weapons being mysteriously missing. Besides when the Agency closed all gun shops, ended all gun fairs, closed all gun manufacturers, shut down all ammo makers, and seized ammo aggressively, what good are the guns with no ammunition. Gun owners saw this as a great opportunity to get some cash while the offer was out there. If you got caught trying to sell a firearm on the internet, on the street, or even to a relative your going to jail for 2 yeas or more. Definitely not worth it. The Agency makes it clear this will be the last opportunity to get cash for your guns. From here on out you only get jail time.

The Agency took in 72 million guns at a cost of 64.8 billion. This is a small number when you compare it to Obama's bank rescue of 900 billion or the Covid Relief packages of over 5 Trillion. Having compensated and closed all the gun dealers, gun and ammo manufacturers, and with no new guns coming in from overseas they really have reduced guns in the U.S. by 67%.

There is a group of survivalists that will never turn in their guns. They don't commit robberies or shootings in south Chicago. They are collectors that have expensive show pieces that they rarely fire that are really just hobby guns. They don't do school mass shootings. And there is those that still feel a need for a gun in the house for protection. That's OK, they normally don't rob mini Milesets. Someone had to go out and get backup ammo real quick when the ammo grab happened two years ago. The ammo is worth more than the gun.

The goal was to reduce shootings, deaths, suicides, and violent crimes, This has been achieved, especially in the drug infested inner cities. The drug business and territory wars are over. South Chicago is as safe as the Miracle Mile.

This was another good reason for decoupling with China, they love to sell the US Fentenol and guns. The CBP also check any remaining cargo arriving from overseas with a fine tooth comb.

Countries found trying to smuggle ammo into the US are usually banned from further export to the US and their governments typically take the criminals that break these export laws to the town square for beheading s as a show of force.

Law enforcement still gets about 8,000 guns a year by stop and search or random stops where people forget to take a gun out of their glove box. The Agency insures that these mistakes by ordinary citizens get publicized. These seizures usually result in 6 months detention and your certainly not getting cash for your gun. Plus your PVR rating is destroyed forever. This will cost you thousands of VC over the years, higher interest rates, and poorer job selections.
Just not worth it !

Chapter 47 – US Peace Corps

Much of the Agency's agenda is shaping the youth of the country for the next American Chapter. They have invested in trade schools, Charter Schools and Public Schools, after school educational programs and athletics, the arts, drama, and music. Clubs abound around the communities for youth with the same interests. They have installed a sense of contribution and public service in the new youth. They are taught very young that service and contribution to community result in better college opportunities, a better PVR (Personal Value Rating) which also means better job placement and more freedoms. Benefits like overseas travel and preferred reservations to high demand vacation spots, more pay, better housing and a whole list of perks and opportunities. One of the best ways to improve your PVR is to sign up for the Peace Corps, a minimum 3 year obligation. Youth completing their minimum study and achievement levels often by 16 or 17 are eligible. Service in the Peace Corp has a variety of further education and responsibilities. The Peace Corp goes into under served communities and mentors children. They teach theology and religion, organized sports, tutoring, survival skills, outdoor appreciation, animal husbandry and agricultural concepts. They rescue pets and other animals, nurture injured or abused pets, and find placement homes. They are a favorite organization for Peta and the thousands of humane societies. They clean up and maintain parks, trails, waterways while learning ecology. Those with mechanical skills volunteer their time doing plumbing, electrical, carpentry, landscaping, painting, and safety mitigation; especially in impoverished areas. Some join the HAC teams working on new planned communities. They run summer camps and community recreation. They all receive competitive compensation as their first step to financial independence.

They make lifelong friends, many fall in love and get married in the Peace Corp. The program has been praised internationally and copied by many countries as the best stepping stone from primary education into adulthood.

Chapter 48 – The Whole Agency Portfolio

About 2033 the Agency began selling off companies to the private sector. It was the plan from the beginning the Agency filled the pipeline vacated by closed borders and isolation. Often they purposely created these companies to be 50–150 employees with sales of 5 million to 100 million VC. This was so they were affordable bargains to be acquired by other industry leaders at some point. The Board of th Agency already had enough money for 30 lifetimes, 100 lifetimes, They wanted more entrepreneurs to succeed. In about half the sales or transfers the employees purchased the companies under favorable terms. Gifted by their hard work and loyalty, these early pioneers in the new economy would retire young with better than good financial security and incomes. The Agency portfolio was comprised of a network of subsidy corporations, about 900 at the latest count. Some as big as the CAH Corporation for American Health which with the HAC , Home America Corporation would continue to be stock holder and stakeholder owned. Companies of the people and the government forever. They were to vital to the American people health and primary need, housing, to ever let a corporate board sell parts, break them up, or do something stupid or greedy that would endanger their existence. The VC, now the world currency to some extent, that originally was valued at less than one dollar to one VC has 25 folded it's value in the past 10 years. If you wanted to buy a home on the coast of Nice that sells for 1 million Euro you can buy it with 40,000 VC. About ½ years typical pay. An espresso in Paris is .20 VC. A imported car previously 150,000 VC can be purchased for 8,000 VC if it's allowed in the US.

The poor investors that had to take.50 VC for their treasury notes and bonds have made out like bandits. Investors in Agency stock have seen 10 fold increase in value over the decade, that's even with 80% of the Agency income getting reinvested into the infrastructure of the communities. The Agency paid down the national debt to zero. The US now owns outright their 8,000 tons of Gold being held in national banks and Fort Knox.

The U.S. doesn't rely on any foreign nation. Never again. We call the shots when it comes to UN decisions, the middle east, the environment, favored nations, and agencies like the WHO.

Not that anyone would wish failure on anyone else but the greedy Chinese is now the weakest large economy in the world. Most of their billionaires and millionaires now have to work. Food is like gold. Their military is sorely depleted.
Their ranking in technology, now that they can't steal from our universities and companies, is in the tank. After the Australia showdown that havn't once tested the will or might of America.

The U.S. is producing 30% more energy than they could ever use. While wind farms never met the cost vs. benefit test, solar was everywhere. New Homes, commercial buildings, manufacturing plants, automobiles, public transportation, farm equipment, had gone 70% solar. Battery technology had reached the point tht a farm harvester could work all day on one charge. Vehicles could travel 600 miles on a charge and recharging only took about 45 minutes. Home storage batteries had become the least expensive construction expense in new single family residences at around 3,000 VC with systems that could hold a five day supply of energy. The 10 year cost of being 100% solar was about 80 VC per month, easily ¼ the cost of traditional public utilities. Elton Misker had overtaken Alan Blake as the richest man in the world with his battery and system patents. His net worth was over 800 billion VC. He was a major Agency supporter and consummate philanthropist. Hi speed rails with luxury dining and entertainment including live performances and movies moved people from New York City to Miami at 230 miles per hour, in 4 ½ hours. The real jewels of the Agency were the home building and medical industries.

As they divested themselves from the various industries they created or bridged supply chains over the years, the proceeds returned to the general fund and the Agency corporations paid the traditional 5% ofn the gross sales amount of the companies. Nobody escaped the 5%. As a result by 2038, shortly before the reintroduction of the new US Congress, the Agency approved a one time payment of 10,000 VC to every America. A family of four got 40,000 VC, Normally economists would suggest massive inflation with such a move. The Agency was well advised that with the supply chains running at 150%, no reliance on foreign manufacturers, ports, or imported oil, that the influx of cash would certainly create demand but that the outcome would be larger corporate profits and larger revenues for the Treasury. Families could save the money, invest it, buy a car, or even take a vacation. These windfall was touted as, you worked, you complied, you helped your neighbor, you were faithful to your principals, and you deserved it; better you spend it than the Agency.

Chapter 49 – Freedoms slowly coming back to

Americans

With the re-election of Don Jr. in 2029, remember the elections were delayed by 6 months in 2024, the American people were policing themselves for the benefit and support of the Agency. It was very unpopular to speak poorly about the Agency and dissenters had to stick together. They were a small minority. With crime about as low as it would ever get and with rehabilitation so successful, the borders being shut ironclad and no new terrorists threats, the Agency decided to show their good and promised intentions of restoring many freedoms.

- Guns were not coming back but law enforcement would not go out of their way to find guns and prosecute
- Speech, the press, rallies, the internet should feel free to express themselves in any lawful way, although mobs and violence would not be tolerated
- Overseas travel would be allowed on a lottery basis, only 2000 Americans at any one time with destinations, purpose, overseas contacts and firm return dates mandatory.
- Overseas visitors would be allowed in thje same numbers, about 2000 at any one time, only from selected safe countries,

- Couples could choose their own mates and

life partners with no DNA sequencing and have children at their own time and choosing
- Quotas and restrictions on most occupations were lifted and with few exceptions people could move freely from job to job
- Mandatory 3 year public service was lifted but still highly recommended as a path to higher PVR and success

Chapter 50 – Russia capitulates and Iran sent into the Dark Ages

Without the Raw Tiber contract with Russia from 2025 the Agency and the American people would have struggled to reach the heights of success. The move preserved our Pacific Northwest and other forest habitats while offering and almost endless building supply. More than 18 million board feet of lumber was imported for 10 years in log form and then milled to order in Alaska, Oregon, Washington, and California. This also added 40,000 high paying jobs to the timber industry, In return the U.S. gave favored status to Russia for commodity crops like wheat, corn, soy, and even American Beef to feed it's masses. Such timing. It was just when we had decided to decouple from China so Russia filled the void in exports created by our decoupling. Russia also purchased license to operate the technology of our VC card system. Many other smaller deals were struck with open support from the Russian consulate general and the Agency. Our newest best buds kept promises to back down on any desires to grab territory or influence in Ukraine or Eastern Europe. Don Jr and the new Russian President Alex Troposky had many more things in common than differences. They both were involved in transformational parties and policies. Their kids were about the same age.

They both loved the outdoors, hunting, and playing chess. It was such a turn around from the cold war days of past.

In Iran the Ayatollahs squashed revolutions in 2027 and again in 2030. They killed thousands of citizens and cracked down even harder on any western ways. They tried in 2028 to bury Israel in over 5000 rockets that were smuggled into Gaza and Lebanon. The Israeli's barely defended themselves before begging the U.S. to get involved. The Iranian's had completed enriching uranium to weapons grade and the U.S. spies and ears on the ground had located 5 launching sites with intercontinental ballistic capabilities. A tough decision and one the Don Jr would only make with the blessings of the Agency; following the two week barrage from both Hamas and Hezbollah and some Iranian rockets from Syria Don Jr. ordered Centcom to prepare a drone only assault on all Iranian sites believed to contain nuclear capabilities. The Space Command plotted attack routes and strategic targets for about a week and gave the all ready signal. Drones of every size with every possible ordinance flew from aircraft in the Persian Gulf, Oman, Saudi Bases, Turkey, and the Indian Ocean. Over 1200 sorties in two days. They first hit any Iranian air force bases and took out any fighters. Then they took out the short range missiles that could hit Israel which already began to launch.

Then came the big guns. B –52"s loaded to the max with the deadliest, mass destructive bombs and many Mother of All Bombs. They leveled under ground bunkers and uranium production facilities. As thier military unearthed the entrances and exits to these facilities we hit them again, and again, until there was no further action or attempt to rebuild or salvage anything that was left. We certainly got them all or they would have taken any retaliatory strike they could.

Finally the Europeans, Russians, and other countries, exception China, got in lockstep with the U.S. and cutoff all diplomatic ties, froze assets, and cut off all shipments into Iran. Further they refused any Iranian load of Oil to enter their ports. That just about did it for Iran. Unfortunately many Iranians starved or were murdered by the military but at the end of the day, the revolution succeeded and a democratically elected government was accepted throughout the world. They were forbidden from any military purchases, sales, or military training in the future as part of their acceptance back into humanity.

Chapter 51 – Congress reinvented and the 4th Branch

The Agency had picked July 4th 2038 as the day they would return some limited power to the Congress, Supreme Court, and the Executive.
In order to make this momentous day the Agency with the States needed to schedule election for May 2038 and they would give candidates about 3 months for campaigning. Campaign expenditures could not exceed 250,000 VC per candidate regardless of the source. This insured everyday citizens could run for office and not be disadvantaged by super pac's. Here were many of the new rules and actual amendments to the constitution which would not be voted on, just enshrined by the Agency.

- There will be 100 members of the Senate, 2 from each statehood
- There will be 200 congressional representatives, each representing an equal number of population, regardless of their state of residency
- Political parties must register with the Agency and submit signed petitions by at least 30 million members
- Candidates are limited to internal or external campaign funds of 50,000 VC.

Cheating will disqualify candidates
- The elections will be June 15th with a swearing in on July 4th
- The Agency will be the new 4th branch of government and the Agency's powers will set out and subject to change by the Agency itself.
1. The United States is not allowed to enter war or conflicts without the approval of the Agency'
2. The Agency will maintain majority ownership and control of the CAH Corporation for American Health, and the HAC , Housing for America Corporation. The Federal Treasury will pay all tax receipts, that's 5% of the selling price of Real Estate to the Agency for the continued maintenance and survivability of these two corporations.
3. The AC will continue to be the accept currency of the United States and no other currency will be issued.
4. The rules of the AC will survive any legislation or court ruling
5. Immigration quotas will not exceed current levels
6. Travel in and out of the U.S. will maintain at it's 2038 levels
7. The Peace Corp will survive in perpetuity in it's current role.
8. Gun, Ammunition, production and sales will

remain illegal. Imports of either are banned and no government branch shall make changes to these laws.

9. Agency founders, board members, their agents or affiliates are immune from prosecution.

Chapter 52 – Dessert World grows from the Cacti

In 2023 Disney, Universal, Del Webb, Lennar, Citation, two baseball franchises, and a group of smaller investors were in talks with Maricopa Regional Planning in Arizona. They were envisioning a destination resort of 64,000 acres, 10 square miles. It was to be located at the foot of the Superstition Mountains in Apache Junction. Elton Misk entered the talks and planing in 2024 and pledged 80 billion in investment. They were talking about entertainment venues:

- 6 Disney Parks
- Universal
- Seaworld
- Westworld (A new theme park)
- Six major resort hotels
- Many smaller hotel lodges
- A convention center
- A new airport
- 8 – 18 hole golf courses
- A large outdoor amphitheater to hold 25,000
- 4 Casino resorts

- Lakes (with no alligators), Bike paths, walking paths
- Water sports, water skiing lakes, jet skis, para sailing, fishing
- A Zoo
- Interactive environmental exhibitions
- Three entertainment districts with about 100 restaurants
- And a monorail connecting everything with no fares

Resort parking would be underground. The themes would be a mix of Dessert, Polynesian, Asian, American West and Mountain Forrest. Ten Builders would offer from 800 sq foot town homes to 8000 sq foot mansions in gate guarded communities. The planned communities would have Monorail stations and several shopping and dining venues. The Monorail extends to Gilbert and Tempe where parking is available for 10,000 cars and takes you to any theme park, shopping venue, golf course, the airport, or the convention center. A high speed train from Los Angeles connects to the Monorail and whisks travelers from LA to Phoenix in 2 ½ hours. You can get on the train at 6 AM, have breakfast and arrive in time for the 9 AM park openings. The Monorail will eventually connect the four corners of the Phoenix valley and Tucson. The master plan would employee about 120,000 in the construction phases and 90,000 when completed. The finished project would be home to 73,000 permanent residences and snowbirds and attract 130,000 daily visitors.

With the new affluence of working families, near zero unemployment, the ban on overseas travel, this will relieve an over burdened tourist industry in Hawaii, both Coasts, Orlando, and the National Parks. Space and vacation packages for Dessert World started selling out 18 month before the opening in July 2031.

Chapter 53 – The Agency's 2036 State of the Union

After announcing the new freedoms law and the plan to reinstate Congress, the Supreme Court, and expand the Executives power in 2038, the Agency planned a gala State of the Union address and celebration for all America. It would be on July 3, 2036 and part of 4 days of festivities. Alan Blake decided it was time to divulge the origins, members, and motivation of the Agency. There were two major political parties, the Republicans and the Freedom Party. The remnants of the Democratic party couldn't get enough signatures to get on local elections or the 2038 Congressional ballot. The Republican party was the party of the Agency. While some Republican members were skeptical back to 2025, after the turnarounds in the quality of life. The fairness employed for all races, all the new wealth, overwhelming public approval, and even the support of the mainstream media. The Freedom party which loathed the restrictive, totalitarian nature of the Agency was always citing the unconstitutionality of their very existence, that their takeover was a coup deserving of a counter coup, and the perpetrators of the Agency should be tried and put in jail. They were made up of a mix of survivalists, NRA members, Civil Rights activists and Scholars, and many College Professors.

They now met openly and spoke freely although most of the country wouldn't give them the time of the day.

The Board of the Agency was seated at a long table on a raised stage at the foot of the mall. Any surviving original members and the current members were in attendance. They started the ceremony with the playing of the national anthem. There were about 140,000 people that showed up for the event and it was broadcast on every news, radio, and streaming show to America and the world. The MC started by thanking Americans for joining the celebration and for their enduring American spirit and ingenuity during the last decade. He introduced the members starting with Alan Blake and ending with the newest board members. He then turned the mike over to Alan Blake.

" It's been a very trying and interesting time the

past 12 years in America. We, the board, and all our supporters and fiends, are so proud of the American people who have risinen to the occasion and challenge of creating a better life for all ethnicities, all colors, all beliefs and religions, and all peace loving and law abiding citizens. You have shown overwhelming compassion and respect for all people. You are the envy of the Free World. In 2020 myself and some close friends and business associates were deeply concerned about the direction of our country. Between the division among the citizens, the efforts by some to divide us even further, the stalemates in our government and representatives, the unchecked crime and hatred, the failed economic system, and the lack of direction and waste in our bureaucratic systems. Our primary concern and efforts surrounded crime. We now are one of the safest places in the world. We have conquered mental illness to a large extent. We have reinvented rehabilitation and have the lowest rate of recidivism in the world. We are a nation of second chances. We help in world crisis whenever we can afford to but do not and will not force our way of life on any country or civilization. We have almost no troops overseas, our deaths on the battlefields of the world are zero. Our money is spent on human infrastructure, not bullets.

Our economy was is dire straights. He had spent our way into insolvency and we were clearly headed for a devastating collapse as never seen before. With mush regret we had to default on much of our national debt and start over. Our VC system has been praised worldwide and become the new standard for financial systems and equity. Everybody is entitled to a good job, a meaningful and rewarding career, and is compensated fairly so that all Americans have the highest standard of living. We care for our disabled, our Veterans, and those that cannot supply the means of good shelter, food, and security. But we all contribute. There is no free ride.

Our advances in education now have us in the top five of the world. We are leading in the development of medicine and cures and every American receives equal and fair medical treatments and service. Every American can achieve any level of education their dreams will inspire them to. We compensate our professionally trained blue collar services at the highest level and are grateful for their attention to detail, safety, and creative beauty that flowers our cities and landscapes. I visited Dessert World this past month and have never been so in awe in my whole life, you have to go.

I want to give other board members a chance to speak. I just wanted my fellow citizens and devoted family members of this great society to know, how proud I am of all of you today. And now I thank you for your cooperation and trust the past decade plus. Go have some fun ! "

Board members offer similar praise for the American people in turn, with many getting choked up as they spoke. Many thanking and praising Alan Blake for putting it all on the line when there wasn't a lot of hope and giving up his own personal endeavors for the America he so loves.

Chapter 56 – Climate Control and the end of Civilization

Breaking News.....The world didn't come to an end in 2030 as AOC and the climate alarmists had predicted. If anything the quality of the air and water had even gotten 30% better the past decade, despite China and India's ignoring all reasonable constraints at polluting. China's emissions went down considerably as their economy tanked and their factory productions decreased by 60%. A non political and international panel of renowned scientists were empowered and supported by the world community in 2023 to conduct an ongoing study of the environment, investigate and report any patterns, and make recommendations to further the slowing of climate change.
In 2029 they released a report of findings. The earth was experiencing a normal and predictable shift in the tilt as it relates to the Sun. They

documented that this has been going on since the beginning of the earth and we were possibly in the 1000th phase of these shifts. Before the axis begins to move back to favor a more direct alignment with the northern hemisphere, the earth will tilt further to the south by 5 degrees over the next 1500 years. This will result in a probable migration shift from the northern hemisphere to the south.

Another words, if you live in Canada start packing your bags for Brazil in about 3025.

The actions taken by most civilized carbon producing nations were having a measurable and positive effect in normalizing the balance of atmospheric chemicals. Continued transformation to renewable energy sources should be proactive but there was no immediate or near future threat to the atmosphere, ozone layer, or the species. Anything occurring in climate, regional weather such as droughts, storms, fires, earthquakes, or rising water levels would have happened under any circumstances as part of the evolution of the planet.

Chapter 57 – A colorless society

Since 2035 every person living on American soil is an American Citizen. The Agency's mandate of amnesty, pay for your citizenship if you came here illegally or legally, learn the American way, and assimilate into society. The government, federal and local, no longer offered publicity, websites, or forms in multiple languages. English is the American legal language,; Learn it, Get Help, or Maybe Move.

We all have the same education, medical care, and opportunities. No affirmative action is necessary. Caucasians are the minority. There are no illegals, no one is in hiding, everyone has the equal ability to own a home, pick their school, or worship where they want. The race baiting of the 2000's, 2010's, and 2020's was abhorrent. Fueled by a press and overly liberal agenda that had nothing else good to support, the American people saw it for what it was. They tuned out the race argument and took away the liars place in the town square by just ignoring it.

Chapter 58– Congress is reseated

The freedom party won 18 seats in the house out of 200. Independents won 52 seats and 130 went to the Republicans. In the Senate 2 Freedom Party candidates won, 8 Independents, and 90 Republicans. The Presidential election was the year before, always on an odd year now since the assassination of Donald Trump and having got moved to an April election. Out of nowhere, the normally very quiet Barron Trump, just turned 35 in 2036 ran for President and won. His nieces and nephews plus Ivanka, Don Jr, and Erics kids were running the Trump empire.

Barron was a conservative but like his Dad and elder brother, Don Jr., had a compassion and generosity like no other. He was a popular figure and won by 30 points over his Freedom Party rival.

Now with a little more power awarded the Executive, he maintained his primary responsibility was world affairs, diplomacy, and world peace.

He still consulted with the Agency board on almost all matters. Most of the founders and their heirs had close ties and relationships with the Trumps and shared equal values.

Congress was given a budget, about 2 Trillion VC, and was expected to continue to fund the existing programs and have some latitude,

but they could not exceed revenues under any circumstances. The days of printing money or postponing liabilities was no longer. If you didn't collect it, you can't spend it. The Corporation for American Health (CAH) and Housing for Americans Corporation (HAC) were off limits. The Agency got their 5% of RE sales contribution plus their annual income from operations to run these programs exclusively.

The future looked very bight for Americans. The United States had become the model society. With no influence or pressure from the United States,

Dictators and Totalitarian regimes around the world were being replaced by open societies without coups or insurrections. That 1950's mentality of spreading democracy and fighting communism with guns was not necessary any more. Even North Korea reunified as one and were quickly becoming the new Vietnam taking over much of the worlds assembly line production and manufacturing. The world got together every 2 years for the Olympics to celebrate the finest athletes in the world, settle their differences on the playing field and join hands in common principles.

Epilogue

Just before I was headed to the Engineering Academy in Fort Wayne Indiana my parents through a goodbye party and celebration in my behalf. I placed in the top 5% of my secondary school and had received about 15 PVR points for my participation in the Peace Corps, our church, and the mentoring program at our local orphanage. I will have two semesters before I need to commit to my major which I think is going to be agricultural chemistry. I hope to travel someday and agricultural cooperation among nations appears to be a field that involves overseas assignments.

I am yearning to spend some quite time with

Grandpa Trevor today. He had been so instrumental in my development and I always walk away from our talks so much more aware of the little things in life. After all the guests have arrived and everyone is centered around discussion by the Bar B Que, I grab two beers and invite Grandpa Trevor to join me on the far side of the yard. He can tell were headed for one of those sessions of back and forth opinion and me picking his brains for information. We started with a lighter discussion about what college was going to be like, should I work part time, did I have enough money, how often would I be home ? Not long into the discussion I begin speculating what changes might be in store when the Congress is reinstated in 18 months. He suggests that we might not see big changes because the policies and success of the Agency had been so overwhelmingly accepted no one wants to risk going back to the old days.

I ask him what he thinks caused the rise to power of the Agency and what would have happened had they not stepped in. He explains it like this. " Mankind is tribalistic by nature. Gathering nuts, hunting Antelope, and sending a man to the moon were all achieved by communal team efforts. Outcomes have always been better when mankind cooperates and uses all physical and mental resources. In World War II the whole American tribe came together. The men going off to fight the Nazi's and the woman building airplanes, uniforms, and guns. After the 9/11 attacks there was very little discussion about which side of the political spectrum you were on. We were attacked and lost lives of all colors, races, genders, and political ideology. We became tribal and had a goal to bring the perpetrators to justice and never be so vulnerable again.

The ideological and political arena was greatly fueled by the press and especially this new form of communication which started about 2004 and open to anyone, social media.

Very one sided movements, like the universities, the press, and some anarchistic groups got center stage attention in the 2000's and 2010's and picked their moments to fight based on racism, economic equity, and wokism. The middle of the country also characterized as the working men and women, the evangelists, suburban or soccer Moms tended to be Independents. They could be swayed in either direction with a high value on economic security, morals, and things affecting their life's and families. The liberal, somewhat socialistic, vocally loud, and very pissed off faction of our bigger tribe pushed a little too far for these independents and created a lane for a strong, in your face new leader in 2016; The time was right for Donald Trump. He was extremely successful in what he promised and did not deviate an inch from his core beliefs. His followers were as loyal as you get. The press and the liberal left just didn't dislike him, they loathed him for his arrogance, ego, in your face attitude and his well honed ability to debate and win arguments. Worse yet he had successes in bringing some level of peace, stood up to Iran, North Korea, China, and Russia, who all feared and respected him. He shamed the EU for ripping us off and made them come to the table with promised funds.

He put and end to many bureaucracies, cut through red tape, got results, persuaded industry to fulfill his wishes and worked around a congress that otherwise should have kept him silent. His outgoing and brash style was too much for some voters in the middle and he lost his reelection in 2020 by about 5%. This opened the door for socialism under the new regime which bowed to the far left's alter of radical ideas. Within months the middle, independent voter, that moved away from Trump to what they thought was a moderate agenda got buyers remorse. The new liberal left under Joe Biden screwed up anything they touched. A fresh round of civil unrest started up in the fall of 2021. The lines of ideology stiffened as Americans were forced to chose sides between conservative Trumpism supporters and radical change Trump haters. It was tribalism at it's peak of destruction. The Agency founders saw this coming months earlier. Added to that the Biden regime wanted to pay our indebtedness with more indebtedness and the cost of basics was headed the route of Greece and Venezuela. We were going from a place where people could afford necessities and some expendable indulgence to an scrambling economy of grab anything you can while it's available.

This effected families the most. The ability to put food on the table, pay the bills, and save a little for college education was no longer in reach. The Agency's acceptance by the general populace was overwhelmingly high because they promised hope for law and order and a return to a normal standard of living.

"Grandpa, what do you think would have happened in the Agency didn't step in? "

That will be the subject of debate for years. And books, and movies.
One can only speculate. Maybe everything would have just quieted down? Maybe the conflicting sides in government learned to compromise.? Maybe some economists figured out how to unbury us from debt? Maybe the press and social media would have put away the race card? Maybe we would have found a way to deal with poverty, unrest in the world, terrorists, and the surge of migration? Maybe we rethought the urgency to kill fossil fuels and got gas back to 3 AC a gallon and home heating under 400 AC a month? That's a lot to ask for or imagine.

It's possible that a less honest national hero rose from the blue; kind of like Castro in Cuba in the 50's. We could have gone communism and looked a lot like Cuba or Venezuela right now. It's not impossible to think that Americans would have picked their sides and fought it out like the Civil War. Gun sales exploded in the 2019 to 2024 period shortly before the takeover. Everyone was armed to the teeth. You could have seen a mass exodus of American wealth to Europe, South America, and Islands offshore as citizens realized their wealth could be easily taken. Is it possible that everything would have returned to normal had the Agency done nothing?

Yes. But very slim. Even if everyone had a Kum Bah Ya moment the national debt wasn't going away. I can't imagine under what terms the Treasury could pay the interest and still fund the government. You would have had to almost eliminate Social Security, Medicare, Medicaid, Pensions, Safety Nets, cut the Military and much, much more. It would have been more painful then Greece or Venezuela and there would have been an economic uprising from the middle class. We will never know the "what if's" , but the ending of this chapter in American history turned out pretty sweet.

Just remember this Grandpa concludes, " In a tribalistic society the smallest denominator of importance is the family. You have a great one.

Your headed off to college and a new life, your parents are doing great, and I'm going fishing tomorrow !."